THE

VOYAGES & SOJOURNS

OF THE

LADY FROM TOLEDO

THE LADY
FROM TOLEDO

An Historical Novel in Santa Fe

Fray Angélico Chávez

Illustrated by the Author

Friends-of-The-Palace Press
Santa Fe, New Mexico

New material copyright © 1993 by the Museum of New Mexico
Foundation
All rights reserved
Published by the Friends of the Palace Press
P.O. Box 9312
Santa Fe, New Mexico 87504-9312

First Printing

Cover design by R.C. "Doc" Weaver
Cover Illustration by Peter Hurd (1904-1984)
Illustrations by Fray Angélico Chávez
Manufactured in the United States of America

library of congress cataloging-in-publication data

Chávez, Angélico, 1910-
    The Lady from Toledo-An Historical Novel In Santa Fe,
New Mexico/New material herein constitutes a Revised
Facsimile Edition of the original 1960 book; including *"Nuestra
Señora de la Macana,"* by Fray Angélico Chávez (from *The New
Mexico Historical Review*, Vol. XXXIV, No. 2 (April 1959), pp. 81-
97) added at the end of this edition with a new forword/by
Thomas E. Chávez.

This is an unabridged reprint of the original 1960 edition,
published by Academy Guild Press, with new notes, historical
review and foreword.

Library of Congress Number 93-70267

PZ4.C513Lad   CIP
813-C512C

ISBN 0-941108-03-1

IN APPRECIATION

IN APPRECIATION

The Friends of the Palace are grateful to the Museum of New Mexico Foundation for their continued guidance and support.

We also wish to thank the following: R.C. Doc Weaver for his continuing technical assistance with this series of historical reprints, The Museum of New Mexico Press for their valued aid and advice, The New Mexico Historical Review *for granting permission to reprint Fray Angélico's article. . . and most of all a special thanks to the author, Fray Angélico Chávez, for allowing us permission to present this beautiful story to the public once more.*

ABOUT THE AUTHOR

ABOUT THE AUTHOR

Born in Wagon Mound, N.M., April 10, 1910, the eldest of ten children, Fray Angélico Chávez represents the 11th generation of his name in New Mexico. He attended local, public and parochial schools and was educated for the priesthood at Franciscan seminaries in Cincinnati, Ohio, Detroit, Michigan, and Oldenburg, Indiana. Ordained at St. Francis Cathedral in Santa Fe on May 6, 1937, he took the religious name of Angélico after the medieval Dominican frair-painter, Fra Angélico da Fiesole. From 1937-1943 he was a missionary at the Indian Pueblos of Santo Domingo, San Felipe and Cochiti in New Mexico. After a couple of hitches in the Army as a chaplain—which included the invasions of Guam and Leyte, and Occupation Duty in Germany—Fray Angélico resumed his missionary work in the Rocky Mountains. He retired from the priesthood in 1971, after serving thirty four years. He is the author of over twenty books of poetry, stories and history, and is arguably New Mexico's foremost man of letters in the 20th Century. Among his innumerable honors was his recent recognition in June, 1992, by King Juan Carlos I of Spain, who invested him as "Oficial de la orden de Isabel la Catolica." The honor recognizes "sons of Spain who have contributed to the prosperity and good will of the Americas."

INTRODUCTION

INTRODUCTION

*In April, 1959, Fray Angélico Chávez, a writer and historian who
needs no introduction to any southwestern bibliophile, published a scholarly,
footnoted article in the* New Mexico Historical Review. *He wrote about
the beguiling history of a Marian statue known as Our Lady of the
Macana (Nuestra Señora de la Macana). Fray Angélico mentioned that
he had written an historical fictional account of the statue, "in the hope
that it will make interesting reading for wider audiences, if the book happens to find a willing publisher..."*

*Fray Angélico referred to the results of his solid research in which
he investigated the statue's legend, that seemed to have a basis in fact.
As a result, he uncovered a story of New Mexico's 17th century Pueblo
Indian rebellion in which he was able to fill some perplexing historical
gaps. He found in the legend a basis for historical fact, thus verifying*

his belief that "genuine folklore is the poetry of history."

Even more interesting than the unraveling of history perhaps is the novel that Fray Angélico skillfully developed. Six years before the most successful Indian rebellion in North American history, an invalid young girl in Santa Fe was miraculously cured. Her return to good health was said to be a message from her household statue of the Virgin Mary that predicted the impending devastation of the small Spanish colony in New Mexico due to the colonists' poor conduct toward the Catholic priests stationed there. The girl and other survivors of the Pueblo Indian rebellion fled from New Mexico when the prophecy came to pass. The colonists took with them the little statue, which had suffered some damage during the Pueblo Indian siege of Santa Fe.

The statue has survived, first in the mission at Tlalnepantla, Mexico and, then, in various other ecclesiastical buildings in Mexico City, where it is still venerated to this day.

This novel revolves around the miracle of the cure and the Pueblo Indian Revolt of 1680. Here is a story steeped as well as based in history. The Lady From Toledo, is Fray Angélico Chávez's first novel among the twenty three books he has published during his long and distinguished career as New Mexico's most renowned man of letters. As is obvious, a publisher for the novel did surface. The Academy Guild Press of Fresno, California, published the work in 1960. As the original dust jacket of that long since out-of-print book stated:

Where other hands would have padded it out to 600 pages..., Fr. Chávez, with the economy of the poet and the assurance of the scholar, has created a taut legend in which no word is superfluous, every detail lockingly significant—recreating a vital, little-known moment in our country's history.

With singular pleasure, the Friends of the Palace, which is the support group for the Palace of the Governors, the history museum for the

State of New Mexico, has selected this book for the third reprint in its acclaimed series of out-of-print historical novels. The first two are The Royal City by Les Savage, Jr., reprinted in 1988; and The Spanish Bride by Walter O'Meara, reprinted in 1990.

Fray Angèlico's original idea of sharing the enthralling story with a wider audience is exactly the reason the Friends embarked on this program to republish good historical novels germane to New Mexico. The Lady From Toledo is a natural for the series.

This new edition includes Fray Angélico's original illustrations as well as the article, which gives the historical basis for the story. The article was not included in the original edition so the reader will have the special joy of noting just how closely this incredible story is to historical fact.

The proceeds from the sale of this book go into the Endowment Fund of the Palace of the Governors. As you enjoy this book, the staff and Friends of the Palace sincerely hope that your curiosity will be piqued to learn more about New Mexico's wonderful history. We invite you to read our first two historical novels as well, and to visit the Palace of the Governors museum as you strive to learn more history.

It is a great pleasure, through the courtesy of Fray Angélico Chávez and with the permission of the New Mexico Historical Review, to republish this beautifully written and important novel of Santa Fe with the author's initial historical article.

Thomas E. Chávez, Director
Palace of the Governors
Santa Fe, New Mexico

CONTENTS

PRELUDE

PRELUDE

¶ *In the enchanted heart of the great City of Mexico there is a very old stone church, sculptured once by human hands and molded ever since by the fingers of centuries. Its name is San Francisco del Convento Grande. Somewhere underneath the lofty yawns of its age-worn ceiling, or in some nook of what remains of the once extensive friary, may be found the little figure of* Nuestra Señora de la Macana, *which literally means, "Our Lady of the Aztec War Club." The original title, however, was* Nuestra Señora del Sagrario, *which is the ancient patronal Madonna of old Toledo in Spain.*

¶ *This particular figurine is a rather poor miniature copy of the Toledo Virgin; and it did come from Toledo almost four hundred years ago. As such it has no intrinsic worth beyond its* oldness and early arrival in America, for a peek underneath its real clothing reveals, not a fully carved statue in the round, but a plain cone of wood and fabric. It measures less than a foot from crown to toe, so that the bronze pedestal and rayed aureole which were added later, and the wide flounce of the silken dress and mantle, make it look smaller still.

¶ The puny and sad, even mousy, face furthers this illusion of smallness. Not that the little head is out of proportion, for it is well modeled and the countenance has a Spanish doll prettiness. What helps to enliven the sad expression, and draw forth one's sympathy as to a living person, is the realistic bump on the forehead. One cannot help likening Nuestra Señora de la Macana to a sweet little girl who ran headlong into a door, or was knocked on the head by a terrible little brother. Her sacred character has to depend, therefore, on such conventional symbols of the Madonna as the crown on her veiled head, the rococo rays framing her figure, the silver crescent at her feet, and the miniature scepter between her tiny well-formed hands.

¶ But stuck in her midget embrace next to her scepter is an emblem which is far from conventional. It is a strange object of shiny metal, like a key that is almost more teeth than shaft. A closer view shows this instrument to be more like a spear, but with some flaglike projections along the opposite edges of the pole. One has to be informed that this is a stylized miniature replica of a macana, the war club of the ancient Aztec Indians. In reality, the Aztec macuahuitl was a great wooden broadsword, or mace, armed with a flint point and a double-edged row of large flint heads set in saw-tooth fashion. The warrior wielding such a formidable weapon grasped the handle with both hands and swung around with it to mow down whatever stood in its path. The im-

From Toledo

pression it made on Spanish armor in the days of Cortés was remembered long afterward.

❡ All this explains the diminutive Lady's unusual name and,
partially at least, the bump on her brow. For this little image, in
the long ago and under the strangest circumstances, was smashed
to bits by the blow of an Indian warrior's war club. Only, it was not
an Aztec's giant saw-toothed macana that did it, else little of the
statue would have remained to get pieced together again, and to
lend grace and substance to a legend. Actually, the club in question was a much lighter and simpler stone mallet, in the fist of a
Tano warrior from the pueblo of Galisteo just south of Santa Fe
in New Mexico. The pioneer Spaniards of New Mexico referred
to it also as a macana.

❡ How the statuette happens to be so many hundred miles south
in the City of Mexico for centuries now, endowed with such a
peculiarly Aztec weapon and wearing such a realistic lump on
the forehead—this, for long, furnished the material for a most
fanciful and now almost forgotten legend. It started in the year
1683, the year in which the broken little image arrived in southern New Spain following a general revolt of the Pueblo Indians
of New Mexico in 1680, and this is the gist of it: In the far dim
past, the pioneer missionaries of New Mexico took along this
little copy of the Virgin of Toledo; six years before the great
Indian Rebellion there, this very statue miraculously cured a ten-
year old crippled girl, at the same time foretelling the destruction
of the Indian missions and the Spanish colony; the Indians rebelled
under the auspices and leadership of the Devil, who appeared
in the shape of a sinister giant; during the siege of Santa Fe, an
Indian chieftain broke the statue with a blow of his war club—and
was promptly hanged by none other than the Demon himself; all

the missionaries were massacred except one (or maybe two), who fled directly south to the valley of Mexico with the ravaged statue, and there it was expertly restored and cherished with the fondest veneration ever afterward. And, marvelous to say, a wound left by the war club on the Virgin's little brow refused to heal, for always the plaster filling cracked open and fell out whenever some craftsman repaired the forehead and painted it over.

❡ Whatever the apparent historical discrepancies in several details of the legend, not to mention the homely miracles, it is the demonological aspect that principally challenges sober belief. It causes the story to be dismissed as quaint folkloric fancy at best. Yet, as will be seen, it has a solid basis in fact. For, more often than not, legend and folklore are but the foam, the flowering of history. Under the airy froth flow the tides of human life; beneath the fairy bloom run the roots of human experience. By following these currents, tracing these roots, one can come upon the intimate aspirations and sorrows of real people who once upon a time lived and loved and fought, whether for long-range purposes or for the advantage of the moment. Certain periods of history also take on a new meaning thereby.

❡ In the case of the Macana legend, lore and fact come together for what turns out to be more than mere comparison. Not only do the outlines of the seemingly outlandish fantasy fit snugly into the rich contemporary accounts of early southwestern history, which scholars have discovered and edited in our times, but they complement each other, like two plates of a color print. Only a third plate is missing, as it were, one which might have filled out the whole picture by dovetailing with the innumerable dots of the other two. This missing plate, which for lack of further documentation lies well beyond the limited skills of strict historical

From Toledo

scholarship, can only be supplied by the freer intuitive techniques of fiction.

¶ *The scene which emerges depicts the earliest continuous European settlement in what is now the United States of America, and in particular its capital, Santa Fe. It focuses on the mortal encounter of Spanish Christianity with a strong primitive Indian culture, pointing out the remote causes and the immediate agencies that brought everything to a head in the great Pueblo Indian Rebellion of 1680, an event which stirred the soul of Spain and her other New World possessions in its day. Up to now the event has been interpreted from the black-and-white sketches left by governors and captains, as such matters generally are. The human color and intimate details, as experienced by the little folk, Spanish and Indian alike, are provided by the little Lady's legend.*

¶ *From under its froth and flower, and directly from the founts and roots of factual sources, there come these ordinary folk whom conventional history overlooked: obscure aborigines and colonists and soldiers of varied character, friars of obstreperous temperament as well as meek and holy martyrs, a confused Indian warrior with a blood-stained mallet, and, behind it all, a mysterious underground being with memories of darkest Africa simmering in his veins. Though fictional in evocation, their lives are pieced together from swatches and shreds of many colors and patterns, as though these long-forgotten people had left patches of their clothing, of their very skin sometimes, on the cruel brambles of history.*

¶ *And so, this is not primarily the story of the little Lady from Toledo and her Indian war club. She generally stays behind the scenes until the moment of her own prime role at the very climax and on through the anticlimax. But it is really she who brought the whole story together, who holds its diverse elements in place.*

Still, she also proves her own fragile self to be no less intriguing, for managing to survive and preserve her identity through so many centuries when kindred objects have disappeared long since, or else have become anonymous in the ferment of historical and political change.

PART ONE:

THE HIGH SHERIFF'S DAUGHTER

THE HIGH SHERIFF'S DAUGHTER

1. THE WORLD OF DOÑA ANA

The villa of Santa Fe in 1674 had changed little in sixty-four years since its founding in 1610 by Governor Don Pedro de Peralta. The core of certain leading families, like the closely related Romeros, Gómez Robledos, and Luceros de Godoy, had continued residing in the houses built by their founding grandparents, instead of spreading out like the expanding clans of the Bacas, Chávez, and Montoyas, down along the distant unprotected banks of the lengthy Rio del Norte. The Santa Fe citizens also operated cattle haciendas well north of the villa, at La Cañada in the vicinity of San Juan and the other Tehua pueblos; but their main interests clung to the static and sleepy capital; holding the major offices of the kingdom and of its militia had become a habit with them, almost a matter of family heritage. There was no affair at the palace of the lord governor or at the presidio, or even at the parish church, in which some or all of them did not take part.

But little Maria Romero, although her family lived on the plaza, saw little of the meager activities of the villa. In the summertime, if her pains left her for a while, she was carried out to drink in the bright sun, when she gazed languidly—but with a joy that almost hurt—at the great wavy mountains rising behind the dun adobe church towers in quilted patches of deep mysterious green and bright light-hearted emerald. Sometimes the highest peaks wore a delicate mantilla of snow even as late as July.

Or, settled backward on her pallet, Maria stared long and straight into the deep blue dome of sky above, wondering how much further up God and Heaven were, and how long it would take her to fly thither when she died. This thought of dying did not scare her at all; death had sat waiting by her bedside too often to be a stranger, while the heavenly joys he promised to an innocent soul were even now more real to Maria than the few earthly ones she had been able to sample.

Just this past October, for the Holy Rosary vespers on the eve of the first Sunday of the month, she was taken out to witness the torchlight procession around the plaza with the beautiful statue of La Conquistadora from the parish church. The furiously blazing *luminarias* of *ocotl* faggots, marking the line of march all around the great square, were a delight to see. Maria enjoyed most the sight of her father and her Cousin Francisco Gómez Robledo, and Aunt Ana Robledo's two other sons, proudly bearing La Conquistadora on their wide shoulders. Their armor was turned to gold by the series of small bonfires. And behind them walked Aunt Ana herself, looking like a proud and lovely duchess, at the head of the society of La Conquistadora. Cousin Francisco was its presi-

From Toledo

dent, while Aunt Ana was the keeper of the Virgin's wardrobe.

There were other such spectacles throughout the year. Maria missed most of them because of her sick spells, like the Corpus Christi procession last June, when her mother erected one of the altars at their very front door. Then in July, on the feast of St. James, there were games of *el gallo* and *los toros*. But the galloping of horses too close to the houses scared her, and the sight of a live rooster torn to bloody bits gave her nightmares afterward. The game of *los toros*, when a wild steer was turned loose in the barricaded plaza, to be baited by the men of the villa, was just as frightful.

Through most of the long winter, however, Maria all too often lay moaning in her room, her pinched features about as pallid as the greyish whitewash of the walls where the underplaster of mud tried to show through. Her tenth birthday had come and gone, but the shallow outline of her wasted body under the coverlet was that of a much younger child, a lifeless one at that. Only her large brown eyes seemed really alive, if more with the ember glow of suffering than the sparkle of vitality. Maria usually stifled any sounds of suffering. It not only befitted the daughter of a very brave father, she had taught herself to think, but it emulated the ladylike conduct of a certain Lady who once stood silent beneath the Cross. But sometimes the pressure of pain was so heavy that it forced out her anguish in bubbles of thin sound. One could hold the lips tight, and clench the teeth, but not the nostrils; and sometimes the ears felt as though they were letting the moans escape.

It was at these times that Maria most often looked fixedly upon the small arched niche dug in the wall opposite, not far above the level of her eyes. In it was perched a little figure with a tiny crowned head no bigger than a ripe apricot; it was also smooth and pale like one, while her vesture of iridescent blue and pink spread outward like a butterfly's. At such times Maria felt that she kept on seeing the figurine even after she fell asleep from sheer exhaustion. But even on painless days, this was the single attraction in the room. There was nothing else to entertain the eye in the low gloomy ceiling of brown pine *vigas* overlaid with rough brownish boards. The wavy white-to-grey walls all around were just as dull, except for the small oven-like fireplace of whitewashed *adobe* in the far corner. This *horno* did furnish a sweet and fragrant comfort; the cozy cover of air which it threw across her bed was like her dear father's caress. Its smell, with occasional blue spirals of smoke escaping outward from the crackling *piñon* firewood, reminded her of the incense with which the priest blessed her room and every room of the villa on the feast of the Kings in January. To Maria, this *piñon* smoke was like a constant re-blessing of *Nuestra Señora del Sagrario de Toledo* in her wall recess, and so Maria's attention constantly returned thither also in days which brought no pain.

A long time ago, when she first began having intermittent waves of fever and dull aches in her bones, her mother had said that this Lady from Toledo could cure her, if Maria prayed hard enough, and if it was the will of God. However, it must not have been God's will, for, in spite of all her childlike faith and trust, the pains had grown steadily worse, and by now she could scarcely move at all. Now, even breathing was painful work. Aunt Ana Robledo had likewise made scores of novenas to La Conquistadora in her shrine inside the parish church of the villa, but the Holy Mother seemed just as deaf and unwilling in her capacity as Queen of the villa and kingdom.

Good Father Juan Bernal, who was a very dear friend of her

From Toledo

father, and always stopped in whenever he came to Santa Fe from the nearby pueblo of Galisteo, had already told Maria that she would soon die and go to Heaven, where she would see the real Lady in person forever. Maria remembered that there were tears in his small hazel eyes when he asked her to offer up her pains in expiation for the sins of the kingdom, whatever these all meant. He also made her promise to ask her heavenly Mother, the day she saw her face to face, to intercede with her Divine Son for the welfare of the Franciscan custody and its missions. This promise was uppermost in Maria's mind whenever the shocks of pain returned in force. And it helped to make them more bearable, as she fixed her gaze on the little Virgin—that is, if she did not have to squeeze her eyes tight for the pain.

Maria was not always alone, of course. In those days and evenings when she and everybody else thought that she was going to die, her mother and her aunts and her cousins, and other pious women of the villa, all hooded in black shawls, knelt in prayer around her bed. Their murmuring of the rosary had a soothing hum, like gently falling rain. In her good days, Maria joyfully welcomed the long visits of her Aunt Ana Robledo, who told the most interesting and edifying stories about their family since the founding of the kingdom. There were also several girl cousins of Maria's own age who romped around her bed gushing all sorts of pleasant nonsense; Maria loved the sound of their shrill voices, of their laughter like cool water.

Then there was big and strong Cousin Francisco Gómez Robledo, Aunt Ana's eldest son and the father of some of the girls who came to play. He came once in a long while, for he was the busy *maese de campo* or field commander of the colonial militia. His booming presence and his merry voice even gave her strength to laugh with him. Naturally, her own father and mother attended her as only loving parents can, but Bartolomé Romero was often gone from the villa for weeks on end, like Cousin Francisco, on the duties of his own office as high sheriff of the kingdom. Or else he was looking after the distant family hacienda and the Indian pueblo entrusted to his care. Maria missed her father terribly, for, even more than Cousin Francisco, he made her feel so much better by merely coming close.

Josefa de Archuleta did all that a good mother could for her paralyzed daughter. Maria could feel her warm tenderness when she washed and fed her daily, and smoothed her bed, and cleaned the room as neat as the golden bundle of *popotl* straws with which she swept the rock-hard earthen floor. Yet Josefa's presence did not make the sick girl feel any stronger or happier, like that of her father. Josefa herself was bent and thin, her naturally dark complexion about as pale as the smooth stub of wax in front of the tiny Virgin on the wall. There were bluish patches under her sad brown eyes, large and round eyes when the eyelids were not drooping in tune with her narrow shoulders. She spoke little, but sometimes she fell to talking about the family's past, like Aunt Ana, except that she dwelt on sad happenings, or gave a gloomy twist to events which were not so sad in themselves. As a matter of fact, Josefa blamed her daughter's pitiful condition on a very bad governor who had reigned at the nearby palace some years before Maria was born.

Her husband Bartolomé Romero—the third of this name, like his father and grandfather—was an *alcalde ordinario* or council-man of the villa and kingdom at the time. He also was an important captain of the militia. But this meant nothing to Governor Mendizábal. Simply because Romero was a faithful pillar of the

From Toledo

Church, like his father and grandfather before him, and because Mendizábal fiendishly hated everything sacred, this evil governor forced Bartolomé and Josefa to go on some senseless errand to the faraway pueblo of Picuris in the high northern mountains near Taos. It was in October, an autumn of pinching frost that year, and ever much colder as the trail rose higher through those wind-swept canyons. Moreover, Josefa was eight months *en cinta,* and the tilted ride on horseback was very rough, to say the least. Her first baby was born dead as a result, and she remained deathly sick for almost a year after that. Then Maria came some years later, very pale and puny, and prone to fevers almost from the start.

Maria cried the first time she heard this story, but after hearing it retold so many times she did not take it so much to heart, although Aunt Ana said it was all too true when she first asked her about it. Nor did she feel any bitterness toward that bad governor, as did her mother after all these years.

From here Josefa would reach further back into the Romero family history for more sad incidents. There was Maria Granillo, her husband's mother, and little Maria's grandmother whom she never knew. She was the wife of Bartolomé Romero the Second, who was also a councilman of the kingdom in his time, in the days of the famed Fray Alonso Benavides. However, a wicked governor was not to blame for her misfortune. It was a bewitched morsel given by an evil woman, the wife of a certain Griego, to Romero's bride when she was about to have a baby—and all in revenge because Romero had spurned that woman to marry Maria Granillo. This Grandmother Granillo remained sick for a very long time. Fortunately, wise old Brother Gerónimo de Pedraza was still alive and practicing physic at the far southern pueblos of Socorro and Senecú. With her ailing mother and grandmother, Maria Granillo made the long journey to see him, and he cured all three of their several ailments.

While Josefa de Archuleta droned on morosely as she swept the room, Maria in her bed went on thinking about Brother Gerónimo. His memory had remained like a benediction among Indians and Spaniards alike. Maria was sure that he could cure her, were he still alive, and sometimes she prayed to him, for he had been a very holy man. Aunt Ana also spoke beautifully about him, and then Maria remembered a story which Cousin Francisco told her in his funny laughing way, as to how the innocent laybrother was wounded accidentally by the lord governor's pistol when still a young friar. This happened long, long ago in the days of Maria's great-grandparents, Luisa Robledo and the first Bartolomé Romero, both of whom had come from Toledo as first settlers of the land.

This very great-grandmother of Maria's, Josefa would say, had had her own share of suffering. Luisa Robledo was carrying Maria's grandfather, the second Bartolomé, when she made that long perilous trip all the way from New Spain in a clumsy wooden cart. Just as the colony entered the new land her own dear father, Pedro Robledo, died by the Rio del Norte, near a lonely bare mountain far south near Guadalupe del Paso which still bore his name. Luisa was still mourning him, and ailing from her delivery at San Juan, when one of her younger brothers jumped off the great rock of Acoma and was killed. There was no doubt, Josefa would always end in saying, that the women of all the Romeros had been marked for especial suffering and anguish at the time they had their children.

But Maria had also heard the good side of most of these stories from Aunt Ana Robledo, the brave side. And because Aunt Ana

was so brave herself, she greatly enjoyed hearing her tell them
over and over again. It was also the nice way in which she told
them, the crisp clear words leaving her firmly curved little mouth
like a song. And the movements of her thin white hands, laced
with threads of lightest blue, were like graceful birds she had seen
fluttering in dreams. Her crown of fluffy hair, now glossy white
like the glistening spore of milkweed pods that her little cousins
peeled on her coverlet in the fall, had once been golden like new
straws of *popotl*—so people said. And Aunt Ana had such beautiful eyes that twinkled as she spoke; they were rich blue like bits
of turquoise in their chalk-white bed when newly mined from one
of the hills of Los Cerrillos just south of the villa. But they were
also soft and airy like the summer sky above the sierra behind the
villa. They seemed to govern the very movements of Aunt Ana's
slender body, and they lit up her pretty, sharp-nosed, wrinkled
little face—all of seventy years, Aunt Ana herself acknowledged
proudly, simply because she did not look so utterly ancient; Josefa
de Archuleta, perhaps a bit jealous, once remarked to Maria that
Ana Robledo walked and talked like a duchess. Nobody in the
kingdom had ever seen a duchess; it was an expression passed down
from some pioneer colonist who might have seen one in Spain, or
just picked it up from his own elders over there. To Maria it
meant something fine and superior in a woman, and Aunt Ana was
all of that.

Actually, Ana Robledo was Maria's grandaunt, her Romero
grandfather's younger sister. She had kept her mother's maiden
name, instead of Romero, to carry it on as a gesture of family
pride. Hence the double surname of her own Gómez Robledo
children. Gómez was her late husband's name. She did it because
her three surviving Robledo uncles had left the kingdom in its

early years, the fourth having perished most dramatically under the cliff of Acoma. "*Doña Ana*," everybody called her, as if she really were a duchess, a title given only to the current lord governor's lady. But Maria liked Aunt Ana the most for being always so jolly and brave about life, like her own father and Cousin Francisco. She could not help wondering how the little woman had reared such a large family, and still was helping with a score of grand-children of all sizes—among them some of those girls who came to play at her bedside—and yet be so lively and young-looking, not at all like her mother Josefa who was young enough to be her daughter. Maria also wondered how such a slip of a woman could have stood up to such tyrants as Governor Mendizábal and the in-famous Governor Peñalosa. These last stories were told her by Cousin Francisco, for Aunt Ana herself, Maria had come to learn, skipped anything which might not sound or look ladylike.

With all that, Maria's fondness for Aunt Ana's visits and stories —and the little cinnamon sweetcakes she made her munch while listening to her—went beyond her delightful self and one's mere pride of family. No matter what their nature, the tales drifted in a certain direction eventually, and Maria's eyes followed their fascinating course to the recessed niche in the wall across from the foot of her bed. Aunt Ana herself never failed to take down and kiss the little Lady from Toledo whenever she entered or left the room. Somehow, Maria felt, the proud little "duchess" was more than a bit envious of her deceased elder brother, the second Bar-tolomé, for having inherited the prime heirloom of the Robledo family from their mother Luisa.

"She is our only link with the glorious place of our origin," Maria heard her say many a time. This usually meant a retelling of the little Virgin's own story, if no one came in to interrupt. The old

From Toledo

lady usually started with the beginnings of the ancient City of Toledo, which thrilled Maria because of its fairylike strangeness through the mere mention of castles and cathedrals. This was followed by the entire Robledo-Romero saga. The recounting of all of it had come to vary so little that Maria could recall most of it by heart. In the long winter nights, whenever she happened to wake up and could not go to sleep for the frightful night noises, like the creaking of the ceiling *vigas* or the tapping of sleet on the sizzly panes of mica in her window, or else the sneaky scurrying of a mouse along the wall and under her bed, she shut her eyes under the covers and imagined Aunt Ana talking musically by her side.

2. BLADES FROM TOLEDO

"The ancient city of Toledo, my dear child, is the heart of Mother Spain." Thus Aunt Ana always began. "Its thousands of houses cling like thick flocks of white doves upon a very big mound, like the back of a gigantic turtle. The great bluff is almost surrounded by a beautiful curve of the majestic river Tajo. Above the upper houses with their tiled roofs the great cathedral rises like a crown of stone filigree. It is the mother church of all the Spanish kingdoms. My mother, Luisa Robledo, was too small when she left Toledo, to remember. But my widowed grandmother, Catalina López, often described the city to me, for she was very homesick for it. I was younger than you at the time, before she and her three remaining sons left this poor kingdom for the mines of Cuencamé down in New Spain. My dear father Bartolomé Romero also remembered how Toledo looked, for he left as a young man years after my Robledo grandparents came to the Indies. Pedro and Catalina had only two children at the time, my Uncle Diego Robledo and my mother Luisa Robledo. But my father Bartolomé spoke little about the things I am telling you concerning Toledo and our Lady's shrine in its cathedral, because he was from a neighboring town. Besides, most men do not pay much attention to details of this kind.

"In the cathedral of Toledo there is a great chapel, called *El Sagrario.* All Spanish cathedrals have a Sagrario, where our Lord in the Blessed Sacrament dwells, and which also serves as a parish church for the people living nearby. For, you see, the cathedral it-self holds the lord bishop's throne, and it is the church of the whole diocese, not merely of the folk in its neighborhood. Now, in the Sagrario chapel of Toledo's cathedral there is a famous shrine of Our Lady with a very, very old statue of holy Mary, which for this reason is called *Nuestra Señora del Sagrario.* It was brought to Toledo from Rome by the very first bishop, St. Eugene, in the first century of Christianity.

"Grandmother Catalina López told me this Lady's story when I was a little girl, but I remember it more clearly because, as a young woman, I used to ask the wise old fathers of this villa about the patroness of Toledo and her shrine—like Fray Alonso Bena-vides, who was the father custos of the custody, and the one who confirmed my eldest son, your cousin Francisco. Now, a bishop, my dear Maria, like the archibishop of Toledo or of the City of Mexico, is the one who confirms people. But this miserable kingdom of ours never has had a bishop, and so the father custos of our Franciscan custody confers this sacrament with the permission of the Pope in Rome. As I was saying, Father Benavides, who con-firmed my Francisco, and also other old friars I knew, had learned all about the Toledo shrine from books in the library of El Con-vento Grande in the City of Mexico."

From Toledo

(It was most difficult for Maria to conjure up a great city like Toledo in her mind, for never having seen a single white building with a tiled roof, or one of carved stone, or even a large river to match the Tajo. Instead, she pictured to herself all the drab houses of Santa Fe piled helter-skelter over the sides of a big hill, called the Atalaya, which rose at the foot of the great sierra east of the villa. On its top she placed the villa's dun parish church for a cathedral, and then she imagined the little Santa Fe stream roaring in full spring flood around the Atalaya's base. A bishop she could fancy more readily, from the small altar paintings of San Buenaventura and San Luis Obispo in the parish church.)

"My darling niece," Aunt Ana went on, "the original Lady of Toledo is a large seated figure of carved wood, which was covered in later times with thin sheets of silver hammered close against the shape of it. This silver was sent to Spain right after the conquest of Mexico by Don Hernando Cortés. The Holy Child on the Lady's bent left arm is separate and comes off. And both Mother and Child are dressed with material far richer and more precious than the mantles I myself make for La Conquistadora, as well as for your—our—little copy of Toledo's Virgin. This is why the Lady of Toledo in the Sagrario appears as though she is standing. Years ago the colonial militia's field commander, my late *compadre* Don Pedro de Chávez, who was my son Francisco's godfather in baptism, once told me that he recalled a similar Virgin in his own homeland in Spain. Her name is *Nuestra Señora de Guadalupe* because her shrine is in Guadalupe near the city of Trujillo in Don Pedro's native Extremadura, which is west of Toledo and near my late husband's country of Portugal. This Lady is also seated, but looks as though she is standing because of the clothing. As for the Toledo Virgin, she sometimes carries her Son, sometimes not—

Father Benavides once explained to me—depending on the church season, or else the whim of her sacristans.

"St. Eugene built the first chapel for the image he had brought from Rome. Many wise and holy bishops succeeded him down the centuries. Many of them are saints of the church like him, and all of them were most devoted to the Virgin which the first bishop had brought, each one adding to the glory of her shrine. Then Toledo was made an archbishopric. Her archbishops continued adding glory to the ever-aging shrine. Chief and best known among them is the great St. Ildefonso. He not only wrote learned books on doctrine and Holy Scripture, but also a beautiful homage to Mary on her perpetual virginity. Because of it, no doubt, Mary one day appeared to him in person, as he knelt praying before the ancient image of herself. Mary was carrying on her arm the richest chasuble from the cathedral sacristy, and she placed it over his shoulders, as when a bishop ordains a priest. It was to show St. Ildefonso that she considered him her very own priest, her very own archbishop. In doing so, the Mother of God brushed the ancient statue with her person, and this made it all the more precious to her people of Toledo.

"These people, my dear, had long ago abandoned their own heathen beliefs completely, and had become genuine Catholics—not like our Indians in the pueblos who want to adore the true God and to venerate His saints, but at the same time set their prayersticks with feathers before idols inside their *estufas,* or at their secret fetish shrines among the hills and *arroyos.* Not only did our ancestors, the Old Spaniards, become real Christians—they were loving champions also of the spotless Mother of God!"

(Maria did not want to contradict her aunt, even silently, but she could not help thinking that Aunt Ana was perhaps a little

From Toledo

too proud of being Spanish, and Toledo Spanish, if it made her think less of other kinds of people. There were many fine Catholics among the mission Indians, for her father had often told her so, and Cousin Francisco, and also Father Bernal. Some of these Indians, they said, were better Catholics by far than many of the colonists. In fact, there was a Tano couple from Father Bernal's mission of Galisteo whom Maria liked and admired very much; they lived with the Mexican Indians in Analco near the chapel of San Miguel across the villa's stream. Whenever these two Indians came to do some housework for her mother, like replastering the entire house with mud, the kind woman brought Maria a sheaf of tasty *guayáve*, a tissue-thin bread which she made by spreading blue-maize paste over hot stones with her bare hands. She and her husband, Juan el Tano, would then pay their respects to her little Lady in her niche. Maria was profoundly touched by their slow deliberate manner of crossing themselves, and especially by Juan's reverent gesture when removing his bandanna before bowing his head in prayer. But suddenly becoming sorry for judging her beloved duchess, Maria harked back to St. Ildefonso and the Virgin —what a privilege it was to see the living Mother of the Lord with one's earthly eyes! Maria could expand her own little copy of Toledo's Madonna, with the eyes one has inside the head, into a real life-size Lady, enriching her dress and mantle with a generous sprinkling of fancied spangles and brooches of filigree. But still, Maria could not help wondering to what extent the Indian's heathen ways could be the grave "sins of the kingdom" mentioned to her by Father Bernal.)

"You have not been listening, my child! Now pay attention like a good girl," Aunt Ana would say. "Well, hundreds of years ago the fierce Moors invaded most of Spain. They were infidels and

sworn enemies of all Christians. As the Spanish cities were conquered by them, one after another, the people retreated to their
northern mountains; but before doing so, they hid or buried their
treasured statues to save them from destruction. For the Moors
hated images most of all. When Toledo was about to fall into
the hands of the Moslem invaders, the canons of the cathedral hid
St. Eugene's and St. Ildefonso's famed Virgin in a deep well of
an inner patio of the cathedral cloisters. These canons were priests
who wore purple robes, and their duty it was to chant the psalms
daily in the cathedral choir—the way our fathers of the villa do
in our church during Holy Week. They were so scared, those
canons, when they ran away, that they forgot to tell the people
about the statue. Or maybe they feared that some weak Christian,
under torture, might reveal its whereabouts to the enemy. For, you
see, not all the people had a chance to flee. Anyway, those canons
never came back, while the people who stayed in Toledo and the
surrounding country, as Moorish subjects, gave up their ancient
Queen for lost. But they never allowed her memory to fade during
three hundred and more years of Moorish rule."

(If the wild Indians of the plains should ever manage to in-
vade the villa of Santa Fe, Maria would set to thinking, would the
friars bury the villa's statue of Our Lady of the Rosary, La Conquistadora, before they ran off to the mountains? Or would little
Maria herself hide her very own little copy of the famed Virgin
of Toledo? No, she certainly would not. She would face the
foe with it, as did the Lady St. Clare of Assisi, who made the Moorish attackers of her convent fall back in confusion when she faced
them with the Holy Eucharist in her hands. Father Bernal had told
Maria this story last August, when he happened to visit her on
the feast of this valorous woman saint.)

From Toledo

"Well, Maria, our valiant ancestors finally began driving the Moors out of Spain, little by little. It took three hundreds of years of glorious battles to do it. And it is from those famous victories that we have the play of Moors and Christians which our men on horseback put on for St. James' Day in July, besides *el gallo* and *los toros*. After King Alfonso of Castile had wrested the city and province of Toledo from the Moors, the new canons of the cathedral became mystified by strange lights floating like fireflies from the great choir to one of the cloister courtyards. It happened every time the midnight chanting of matins came to a close. Deep in the stillness of night, the lights looked to them like a procession of angels with lit candles, if not one of ghosts. After tracing them to a long-covered well in one of the patios, they investigated the next morning and found the famous lost statue hidden deep inside. You can imagine how the people rejoiced, and you may be sure that there were many grand processions and solemn acts of thanksgiving in the cathedral when they enthroned their ancient Queen of Toledo in the Sagrario chapel. She has reigned there ever since.

"Since then, too, Toledo has been the Mother Church or Primatial See of all Spain, and from that time her archbishops have been cardinal princes of Holy Church as well. But Toledo's chief glory is her valiant antiquity in the Holy Faith, and her famous Virgin is the symbol of it. You can see, then, my darling niece, why I am so proud of my grandparents, Pedro Robledo and Catalina López. And of my dear mother, Luisa Robledo, and my loving father, Bartolomé Romero. May God have them all in His glory. Although none of them, except my mother Luisa, were born in the great city itself, their little native villages close to Toledo were like chicks around the mother hen. The Robledos were from

the town of Maqueda on one side, my Romero father from Cor-
ral de Almaguer on the other. My grandparents lived for a time
in the mother city before making the long journey to Cádiz, where
they took ship for the Indies.

"But when they left home, my mother's family brought a bit
of Toledo with them, your—our—little Lady who stands guard
over your bed night and day. Most every family in Toledo and the
neighboring towns had a copy of the Sagrario Virgin enthroned in
their homes. The rich nobles and wealthy merchants had costly reproductions made in carved wood or metal or ivory, which they
dressed as richly as the original model in the Sagrario chapel. Poorer
and humbler folk bought small images which were not too faithful
copies. Usually, it was only the head and hands that were whittled
out of wood, then covered with gypsum and paint. The body itself was only a hollow frame made of sticks covered with cloth
or leather, like a funnel upside down. But since the image was
to be dressed anyhow, this made no difference. And when their
devout owners moved from one home to another, and especially
if they went away from their native place, they took their native
patroness with them. This is how our little Lady came to this poor
kingdom long ago with my grandparents. And this is why she has
no carved body under her dress, as does La Conquistadora, for my
grandfather was only a poor young soldier at the time."

When little Maria Romero let her mind go thinking along
these lines in the empty black stretches of night, after sleep seemed
to have flown away over the mountains, the envisioning of distant
places and persons and things, which liked to mix with those closer
to home, made the real eyes on her face flare wide open in the

From Toledo

darkness. It felt as though small hard rings were stuck between the eyelids to keep them wide apart. And therefore sleep, which will not allow itself to be seen by anyone, refused to come back from behind the sierra. At the same time, if Maria stopped listening to Aunt Ana's voice, her sensitive ear pressed against the pillow heard a steady padding, like the footsteps of a giant outside. It made her think of fearful giants and evil witches in those fairy tales of the north countries of Europe which Aunt Ana also told her, and which she had heard as a girl from her brother-in-law Gaspar Pérez. This man, now dead many years, had come from the Low Countries and had married Maria Romero, Aunt Ana's eldest sister, the one who came as a baby from New Spain with her parents. Some of his stories, like the one about the piper and the rats, or the one about the beauty and the beast, or even the one about the little girl with a red hood and the wolf that dressed up like her grandmother, were pleasant stories that did not leave a bit of fright lurking in one's head. And this was because they never had been true.

But Maria soon began to think with horror about another giant much closer to home. He was the great black god of Po-he-yemu, whom the Indians claimed lived in the north region of the kingdom and came down at night to peer through the thickest walls with his big yellow eyes. Then, recalling that her mother had told her that the noise of footsteps she heard was only the beat of her scared heart coming up to her temples, Maria straightened her head and the footfalls stopped. But there came again the loud creak of a *viga* overhead, or the gnawing of a mouse from the direction of the cold fireplace. Maria took up listening once more to the voice of Aunt Ana telling about their family and the Lady from Toledo, and she let her inner eyes follow the living pictures that began flashing anew. At last sleep stole back because her eyes and ears went dead limp from weariness while watching the pictures of certain journeyings from the river Tajo to the port of Cádiz, and then a long voyage to the shores of New Spain. It was most difficult to see how a many-sailed galleon looked, for even Aunt Ana had never seen one herself, nor the great ocean sea. But the anxieties and hardships, these Maria did not find hard to imagine.

As Aunt Ana told it, Pedro Robledo and Catalina López had braved the perilous crossing with their boy Diego, born in Maqueda, and their little Luisa, Toledo's own gift, because of a dream in a young soldier's eye. At the barracks castle of San Servando, which looked on the great city over the graceful Alcántara bridge spanning the Tajo's chasm, Pedro had learned much about the ancient battles of Romans and Goths, and of Moors and Spaniards, from retired old sergeants who daily visited the small garrison. Those old battles, no matter how much they excited Pedro's pride for his heritage, were long dead and gone. But there was a not too old veteran from the armies of Don Hernando Cortés who held the young sentinels of San Servando spellbound with his almost incredible tales about the golden conquest of Mexico. His vivid stories about the conquest of Peru by Don Francisco Pizarro, even if he had these only from hearsay, were no less astounding than his own experiences in storming the bloody canals and *teocalis* of Mexico with Don Hernando. And both Pizarro and Cortés had once been ordinary folk from the towns of Trujillo and Medellín directly west of Maqueda, on the same royal highway to the ocean sea which strung Pedro's own birthplace on the same Castilian necklace. This fact brought those fabulous heroes closer to Pedro, made them his very own blood relatives, as it were.

Besides, the days of conquest and military glory in the Indies were far from ended. There was only a pause. For the garrulous veteran had heard of an unexplored mysterious region far north of the fabulous valley of Mexico which even the great Cortés had been forbidden to investigate. Some said that it was out of envy among the nobles of the royal Court. Others claimed that the missionaries had prevailed upon his Catholic Majesty to leave its exploration to the friars exclusively, in order to prevent the inhuman treatment which some of the first Conquistadores had visited upon the natives of the Indies.

This *new* Mexico, fancied by all as a lake-studded valley much richer than the valley of Mexico in the number and size of its golden cities, was said to border on the wealthy kingdoms of India and China. It waited only for his Catholic Majesty to authorize the proper *adelantado* to conquer and colonize it for Holy Church and that could come any day now. Lucky the young men, said the old soldier of Cortés, who signed the muster roles under his banner.

But Pedro Robledo found the New World disappointing from the start, strange and interesting though the landscape of New Spain proved to be with its millions of native inhabitants. The gold of Mexico was all gone; it could still be mined in isolated mountain fastnesses, but only by dint of much hardship and effort, as well as a heart hard enough to impress the native Indians or imported Negroes into what was actually slave labor. The only battles to be fought were gang encounters between provincial adventurers from the different Spanish kingdoms: Castilians against Catalans, Galicians against Andalusians, or all against the Basques—for want of anything else to do. There was plenty of land to till, with plenty of Indians to do the work, but these hardy soldiers of fortune, especially those from the Extremadura of Cortés and Pizarro, had no stomach for it. Their ancestors were knights who had conquered the Moors! What such people were waiting for was the opening of that *other* Mexico in the northern *terra incognita* where each captain would find a dukedom, or at least a small island, to rule.

Less than forty years before Pedro Robledo arrived in New Spain, in 1540, the famed Coronado had led a royal expedition thither, but had returned broken in health and fortune, and also empty-handed. But, after these many years, the general feeling in the streets and in the barracks of New Spain was that Coronado simply had not gone far enough to reach China or India or the Straits of Annian. Then, just four years after Pedro's arrival, three holy friars—Rodríguez, López, and Santa Maria—were sent by the lord viceroy to reconnoitre the land with a squad of escorting soldiers under a Captain Chamuscado. The friars were martyred, the captain died on the way back, the soldiers who returned remained tight-lipped—on the lord viceroy's cautious orders it was said.

It could only mean that there actually were many wealthy cities up there, and that the King only awaited a more favorable time, and the right gentleman, to conquer those realms with the least bloodshed and without antagonizing their superior inhabitants.

And so it was that for more than twenty years the Robledo family had wandered from garrison to garrison in different towns of southern New Spain. Here, in the early years, were born three other sons and another girl, Francisca, the youngest child. Luisa, the girl born in Toledo, married Bartolomé Romero, a countryman newly arrived from Europe and already an *alférez* or junior lieutenant. By now old Pedro was an *alférez* also, if at sixty, after a long empty tour as a *cabo* or corporal. Catalina López, ever home-

From Toledo

sick for her native land, fervently thanked the Virgin of Toledo for at least sending a *toledano* like young Romero to be her eldest daughter's husband; soon these had a baby daughter, Maria.

By the year 1597, Diego, the eldest son born in Maqueda, was a seasoned twenty-six year old soldier in his father's small squadron—while Alonso, the junior Pedro, and Francisco, twenty to seventeen and themselves creoles of the New World, were also well used to their arms—when there came the lord viceroy's proclamation of the Oñate expedition to the new Mexico. Old Pedro's faded dream flamed up like a rekindled dying ember. His four sons, images of their father in more than outward appearance, seconded his immediate decision to sign the lists of Don Juan de Oñate as soldiers and colonists, and so did Romero. They did not need the King's staking allowance, and so could return if the land did not please them, for having gone at their own cost. But there was not the least thought of returning.

Luisa Robledo, also very much like her father, touched her own fire to the enthusiasm of her husband, neither of them pausing to consider the hardships and unknown dangers to which their infant daughter would be exposed. And no less eager was her younger sister Francisca, at her age a mass of daydreams which growing girls have.

"Only my grandmother, Catalina López, was unhappy about joining the colony," Aunt Ana went on. "The dream which had brought her with her dear Pedro from Toledo had now bloomed much too late for her. Besides, she harbored strange forebodings of disappointments and sorrow. All she wanted now was a safe life for

her children and future grandchildren in the presidios of New
Spain, even if there was little hope of bettering their condition.
But her entire family had thought otherwise, especially my mother
Luisa, who always said to me that hardship and sorrow are worth
the search for a better life."

(Maria could hear Aunt Ana's voice grow louder and more
distinct as her great-great-grandparents and their children drew ever
closer to the kingdom. She could easily envision the expedition's
great caravan of ox-drawn carts with wooden wheels like mill-
stones, for she had once seen such a wagon train bringing in the
supplies for the missions and the goods of the new lord governor
and his retinue. She could plainly see the leagues and leagues of
terrible desert that the colony had to cross, the ranges of jagged
stone mountains that it had to manage with all its people and herds,
from landscapes familiar to her eyes closer to home. She could even
imagine what a whole year of such travel could do to body and
soul; for she knew what suffering from heat and thirst meant, from
her own days and nights of fever. And Maria could see Great-
grandmother Luisa Robledo plainly. She looked exactly like her
brave and pretty daughter Ana—that is, as Aunt Ana must have
looked when she was younger. Great-great-grandmother López had
the drooping eyelids and stooped shoulders of Maria's own mother,
Josefa de Archuleta.)

"On reaching the Rio del Norte far south of here, at a point below *El Paso,* or the entrance into this kingdom, Don Juan de Oñate
took formal possession for his Majesty and for Holy Church. My
mother used to tell me that it was a spectacle she never forgot: the
solemn Mass chanted by the friars, and the wonderful sermon, the
happy women wearing their best dresses and shawls and the men
in their shining armor which they had polished for the occasion;

From Toledo

then the drama enacted that afternoon which a captain had composed in order of this *La Toma*, or the taking of the new land for the King; and, above all, the raising with trumpet flourishes and the snare of drums of the new kingdom's royal standard with a picture of *Nuestra Señora de los Remedios* upon it. No, La Conquistadora was not there, for she came to Santa Fe many years later, when I was already married. Our little Lady from Toledo was there, of course, but she lay packed among the household goods in the Robledo cart. I am sure that my dear mother Luisa also rejoiced at the time because she was already carrying my older brother Bartolomé, your own grandfather, who was born months later in the pueblo of San Juan.

"The first real tragic sorrow struck the family when my poor grandfather, Pedro Robledo, died shortly after the colony entered this kingdom, by a large barren mountain which still bears his name. It happened on Corpus Christi Day, and he was the first adult member of the colony to die in the kingdom. Grandmother López was disconsolate; she even berated the day in which she and her Pedro had left Toledo. Naturally, the whole family was also filled with deepest sorrow, but my mother and her brothers felt that this could just as well have happened in New Spain, or even in Toledo, since their beloved father was well on in years.

"Within two months after the expedition's arrival at San Juan, the first mission church was dedicated there. After the Mass there were games of Moors and Christians in which my father and my uncles took part. Plans were also being laid for the first Spanish settlement of San Gabriel, with its own chapel of San Francisco, on a spot nearby where the Rio del Norte and the Chama meet. In the meantime, the Spanish women and their children lived in dark and airless cubbyholes, dwellings borrowed from the San Juan Indians on the second tiers of their mud apartments. In such a swallow's nest was your Grandfather Bartolomé born. I said, the women and children—for most of the men were gone, at one time or another, introducing the missionary fathers to the many pueblos of the region, or else going out in all directions in search of signs or in- formation about harbors and golden cities further on. On one of these expeditions to the great eastern plains over these mountains, my youthful Robledo uncles were the first Europeans to hunt the monstrous bison in earnest. Stories about the risks my uncles took, especially in trying to rope those monsters and bring them back alive, were still being told not too many years ago.

"My mother Luisa also had a chance to show her own bravery, there at San Juan. One day the scouts of the pueblo told Governor Oñate that the wild Indians of the plains were coming to attack the village. They did this every year at harvest time, to make off with the pueblo Indians' maize—as they still try to do, and more often, only that now they come to steal our horses. At that time most of the Spanish men were out exploring for the lord governor, and so Oñate had the alleys and plazas of San Juan barricaded, to be de- fended by the few soldiers left and by the Indian warriors of San Juan. At the same time he ordered the women and children to stay out of harm's way in their upper storeys. My youngest uncle, Fran- cisco Robledo, was placed in command of the first barricade, and we can imagine how Grandmother Catalina López felt—for her baby Francisco had narrowly escaped a terrible death at Acoma shortly before, as I will tell you later on. His older brothers were away from San Juan on a trip of exploration, another cause for worry. Meanwhile, most of the women on the upper terraces had gotten stones together, and pots of boiling water, to throw down upon the invaders. But they were making such a fuss and racket—

From Toledo

Luisa Robledo being the loudest—that Oñate angrily ordered them back into their holes. Instead of obeying, they shouted defiance back at him, and he had to smile with admiration, and so he let them be. The enemy stole away without attacking, no doubt discouraged by the barricades and the few Spanish soldiers who were a complete surprise to them. But the women were given the credit for scaring them away."

(Next came the battle of Acoma, which Aunt Ana sometimes described before telling about the shouting women at San Juan. This account never failed to thrill Maria, the one time she could feel faint tingles along her crippled spine. For the high cliffs of Acoma looming up in her mind made her feel at once dizzy and exhilarated.)

The great pueblo of Acoma stood on top of an immense table of solid rock in a vast desert strewn with similar fragments of mountains many leagues west of the Rio del Norte further down from San Juan. Its beetling sides shot sheer up almost four hundred feet into the blue in some places. The single approach to the level top started in a climb up a steep slope, then went straight up in a narrow winding trail against the walls of a gigantic fissure in the dizzy declivity, ending in a series of hand and toe holds gouged in the wall of living rock. And all this rock immensity was a part of the family saga.

Before leaving with the *alférez* Bartolomé Romero, Aunt Ana's father, and other men to discover the north shore of the South Sea, Don Juan de Oñate left instructions for one of his nephews and a party of thirty men to gather extra supplies for his expedition, and then catch up with him and Romero. This party stopped at

Acoma to look for cornflour and blankets. Their leader led eighteen of his men up the precipice to the village on top, leaving the other twelve with the horses on the desert floor far below. Pedro and Francisco Robledo went up with their leader. But the natives showed themselves unfriendly, sullenly claiming that they had nothing to give in exchange for much coveted hatchets and other tools. All of a sudden, after the Acoma spokesmen had separated the visitors from each other under the pretext of showing them their empty storerooms, the Acoma warriors came out yelling from their hiding places and pounced upon the soldiers. These Spaniards defended themselves desperately, but the small separated groups were no match for the hordes of Indians. Some fell where they stood, while others, fighting at the very edge of the cliff, leaped back into space and fell to their deaths. Thus Oñate's nephew was overpowered and done in while his five companions kept on swinging their swords as they were pushed back steadily to the rim of the precipice, where they dropped backwards into thin air. . . . Among these five were young Pedro Robledo and his younger brother Francisco.

For centuries the desert winds had piled up a big slope of powdery sand at the base of the cliff where these last men jumped down. This deep mattress of dust broke their fall and they walked away alive—all except Pedro, who fell off to one side of it and struck the flinty ground further down. His luckier fellows and the men with the horses fled, leaving their slain comrades in the hands of the enemy, and eventually caught up with the lord governor. Abandoning his South Sea excursion for the time being, Oñate returned to San Juan mourning the death of his nephew. There were further lamentations there among the widows and orphans of the other fallen men, but the bitterest were those of Catalina López over the loss of her second Pedro. Her entire fam-

From Toledo

ily felt her deep sorrow. Even Luisa, ever so proud of her husband, drew little consolation from the fact that Romero had been
promoted to captain for discovering hopeful signs of a river of
pearls that lay on the way to the South Sea.

The punishment of Acoma for her treachery was the next
move, naturally. The fuming brother of Oñate's slain nephew
set out for the cliff pueblo with seventy fully armed men, including a contingent of artillery. Captain Romero and two Robledo
brothers, Diego and Alonso, eagerly went along, as was to be
expected; young Francisco, still shaky from the lucky fall off the
great cliff, was told to stay with his mother for some measure of
solace. Later accounts of the furious battle which took place on the
sky city of Acoma made it rival the most famous encounters in
the Spanish wars against the Moors, as well as the much more
recent conquest of the Aztec capital of Mexico by the armies of
Cortés. It was even said, as being the sworn testimony of some
captured Acoma warriors and chiefs, that the great St. James and
the Holy Virgin Mary had ridden a thunderhead over Acoma
aiding the Spaniards to victory.

Of the more earthly and human feats of valor, the most cele-
brated were those of Diego Robledo, to his sisters' loud gasps
of admiration and the further pain in his mother's breast. Diego's
fierce sallies in revenge of his brother Pedro's death seemed more
reckless than brave, as when he nimbly led the first ten men un-
scathed to the top of the rock through an unbelievable shower
of arrows and stones. There a burly chieftain lurched at him and
Diego, parrying with his sword, ran him through the chest.
Dropping his *macana*, the wounded Acoman tried to grapple with
Diego again and got the sword clear through his thigh. Then,
having fallen prone as if dead, he clutched the unsuspecting Diego

by both ankles, stood up straight, whirled him around a few times, and sent him flying headfirst full six feet away. Only then did this big Indian fall down really dead.

Infuriated by this humiliation, Diego threw himself into the general fray with such madness that scores of the foe fell to his dagger and sword. His fury was still boiling hot after the main battle was over. After he and other soldiers had returned to the camp below, a young Acoma brave, breaking loose from his captors on top of the cliff, made a clean graceful leap to the sandpile far below which had previously saved Francisco Robledo's life. He landed feet foremost in the sand like a spear, and then nimbly took flight across the desert. But Diego, leaping on a horse, quickly overtook him and ran him through with a lance. His brother-in-law, Captain Bartolomé Romero, was also generously commended for his opportune marksmanship in the beginning, when he picked off Indian warriors on the cliff's rim from the ground below while Diego Robledo was busy gaining the top for the first assault. He also distinguished himself later on in hand-to-hand fighting upon the rock itself during the main heat of battle.

(Timid as little Maria was about such things, she got a thrill going over the gory scenes of this battle with the anxious fly-crawling up the face of the towering rock and the soaring grasshopper leaps to the desert level far below. But it was because of the bravery displayed by her great-grandfather and Aunt Ana's uncles, not from any love of death or slaughter. What did fill her with revulsion, and with shame for her own people, was the fact that Governor Oñate punished the Acoma leaders by having their right hands chopped off. It was Cousin Francisco Gómez Robledo who had related this bloody item to Maria, not Aunt Ana, who must also be ashamed of the incident although her little bosom heaved high and fast when describing the bravery of her father and her uncles.)

"All this was too much for Grandmother Catalina López to take," Aunt Ana's voice went on. "For years after the colony had moved to San Gabriel, she brooded over the deaths of her husband and son, and over the unknown perils her three remaining boys had to face in those fruitless expeditions which Oñate kept on sending out into an endless wilderness. Her sole thought was to get back to Toledo before she died. It was like a madness with her. Because the Robledos had come at their own expense, they were not obliged to stay like most of the colonists, and so she was always after her boys to take her away. My mother Luisa told me that Grandmother López no longer seemed to care much about her two married daughters. At that time my dear mother Luisa was very busy in San Gabriel with her fast growing Maria, who had come as a baby from New Spain, and young Bartolomé, born during the first months at San Juan—and then with myself and two brothers coming in due succession there at San Gabriel. My young Aunt Francisca had married a captain by the name of Tapia, all of whose grandchildren now live far down in the Rio Abajo next to the descendants of my *compadre* Don Pedro de Chávez; you do not know them, my dear, for these cousins live so far away from the villa.

"Well, Grandmother López left us finally, sometime before this villa was founded by Governor Peralta, after Uncle Alonso went and found some good mines in Cuencamé far south in New Spain. It was about the same time that Don Juan de Oñate also went back with his retinue, to answer for his cruelty to the Indians of Acoma. So happy was my grandmother to leave this kingdom, and sure of seeing Toledo again, that my mother Luisa had no trouble getting to keep the family's little Lady from Toledo. Mother willed it to my elder brother Bartolomé, and he to his eldest son, the third Bartolomé, who is your father. This is how you come to have her, my dear."

(This is when Aunt Ana always paused for a few moments, glancing toward the wall niche with a trace of that sharp light in the eye's corner which women have when they are jealous. But then the dear "duchess" would heave a big sigh and turn to Maria with her old familiar tenderness. Here the storytelling ended for the time being. If Maria insisted, she then told one of those German fairy tales that she got from Gaspar Pérez, the Flemish armorer, when she was a girl. The rest of the family history: the subsequent founding of Santa Fe and Aunt Ana's marriage to the Portuguese newcomer, Francisco Gómez, with the adventurous part which they both played in the development of the kingdom, all this constituted a new and distinct phase. This phase was much better told by little Maria's own father, or better still by rough and merry Cousin Francisco, since Aunt Ana left out many interesting things. And Maria could guess the reason why.)

3. SINS OF THE KINGDOM

To little Maria Romero, her father Bartolomé and her Cousin Francisco, who were first cousins to each other, were as much alike in shape and size as are two kernels of Indian maize—

that is to say, a black kernel and a red one. They were of about the same age. Both men had the same brawny stance, the same stride and gestures, the same strong and full features even to the identical cut of their nape-long hair and their short beards. But, while the high sheriff's hair and beard were glossy black like a crow's wing, the field commander's were much more fiery than the russet breast of a robin. The one's eyes were a deep quiet blue, the other's were as light blue as his mother Ana's, but devilishly playful. And so the *alguacil mayor* of the kingdom was more sober in the tone of his voice as in what he said, while the *maese de campo* of the colonial militia, always charging his talk with hearty laughter, found a funny side to incidents of the most serious nature, or what Maria thought should be serious. People said that Francisco Gómez Robledo's laughter rang out through the cliffs and canyons whenever he led an attack on marauding wild Indians, and that it shook the savages more than did the Spanish guns.

Maria much preferred her father's presence, of course, when he sat for long spells by her side each time he came home from a lengthy stay at the family hacienda, or the long trips of his office as high sheriff. The warmth of him actually soothed her pain. But she also rose avidly to the less frequent visits of Cousin Francisco, especially if it was one of those periods when her mother Josefa was feeling more low than usual, dwelling overmuch on the sorrows which all the Romero wives were heir to. Maria could see that Cousin Francisco was just as proud of his forebears as was Aunt Ana. But he made these people much more interesting because of certain details which his mother left out of her accounts on purpose. In fact, his best account was one which Aunt Ana skipped altogether, the one involving her mother Luisa

Robledo, Governor Peralta, and Fray Ysidro, when the villa of
Santa Fe was only three years old. The incident also involved
several other members of the growing Robledo-Romero clan, some
of whom were none too savory characters. All that María had to
do, to start Cousin Francisco off on it, was to remark most in-
nocently that Luisa Robledo must have been the sweetest gentle-
woman who ever lived, just like Aunt Ana. Out would come a
burst of rocking laughter, and, riding bareback upon it, the story.

The extensive earthen plaza of the new villa of Santa Fe—
which Cousin Francisco said was named after a villa near Granada
where Ferdinand and Isabella watched the final conquest of the
Moors—teemed with restless citizens, armed officers and soldiers,
early on a summer morning of the year 1613, while streams of
women quietly scurried from every direction toward the parish
church at the upper end of the square. Governor Peralta had called
an emergency meeting at the palace, and everybody knew what
it meant.
  Like other wives of the villa, Luisa Robledo had been fearfully
startled by her husband's early and quick summons while still
in bed; like the other women, also, her first thought was to seek
divine aid. Leaving her four younger children fast asleep on
their floor mats (little Aunt Ana among them), and with but
a hasty suppliant glance at the little Virgin still buried in shadow
within her niche in the wall, Luisa hurried off to Mass. The sight
of Captain Bartolomé Romero—he of the battle of Acoma and
of the river of pearls—nervously pounding the pommel of his
sword as he conferred with other civic leaders in front of the
palace, made her anxious heart pound all the faster, sending flushes
of blood to her head that blinded her wits as well as her eyes as

From Toledo

she stumbled into the dark parish church. Two lit candles flickered like a cat's eyes over the dim altar far ahead, but evidently
the Mass had not yet started. Luisa soon caught the frightened
faces of the shawled women kneeling all over the bare nave, and
turning as one in her direction at the sound of her footsteps on the
hard earth floor. Their total expression was like a plea for some sort
of solace from her, some relief from the tension which held them
in mute terror.

Luisa obliged them in a way which startled her as soon as
it happened. She let out a piercing scream and began berating the
scandalous happenings of the past months which had turned the
villa and the entire kingdom into a hell of injustice and persecution.
Her outburst loosened up the pent-up emotions of the other women,
and the narrow church began resounding with the chorus of their
combined lamentations.

Due to the lingering darkness in the recessed and windowless
apse ahead, no one had noticed that the new father commissary,
Fray Ysidro Ordóñez, had already started to lay out the chalice
cloths on the altar at the very moment that Romero's wife came in.
The untoward commotion made him spin around furiously. His
usually swollen features had puffed redder still when Luisa began
to curse the day that Fray Ysidro came into office. His booming
voice quelled the lamentations immediately, while the main cause
of the disturbance, suddenly brought back to her senses, cowered
in dismay as he in turn let loose a flood of unchurchly invective
upon her muddled head before proceeding with the holy mysteries.

(His grandmother's unholy outburst, Cousin Francisco would
say with jolly relish, was a surprise to everyone. He said that a
friar who witnessed it wrote later how much it astonished the entire kingdom—for Luisa Robledo was "a most prudent woman,

soft-spoken, honorable, and most devout." But she must have been a grand old girl despite her prudence, Cousin Francisco continued, gurgling through his red beard. Maria thought so, too.)

Captain Bartolomé Romero, Luisa's husband, enjoyed the same honorable reputation throughout the kingdom. He was a right-hand man of the lord governor, while equally acceptable even to Fray Ysidro because of his devout qualities and sincere interest in the things of Holy Church. He had often acted as a go-between in trying to resolve their difficulties, and so happened to have a complete grasp of the whole situation. All this he had confided to his wife. It all hinged on Fray Ysidro's pettiness regarding his official privileges and powers as head of the missions and representative of the Spanish Inquisition; there was his wild use of excommunications upon all and sundry, including some of his own really good friars, whenever his will was crossed. What had brought the differences between him and the lord governor to the boiling point was an incident involving, if only indirectly, the husband of Luisa's sister Francisca, Captain Juan de Tapia, and also Luisa's son-in-law, the armorer Gaspar Pérez. It was only recently that this Gaspar, a Flemish newcomer, had married her eldest daughter Maria.

One bright May morning, while Tapia and other officials were idly discussing the best way in which to raise twelve bison heifers which had been captured for Governor Peralta, the latter came up and thanked them for their interest; then he announced that he was sending Tapia and Pérez with some soldiers to collect a delayed tribute from the pueblo of Taos. As an officer and as the scribe of the *cabildo* or council of the kingdom, Tapia felt free to remonstrate with the lord governor. The date set for the departure happened to be on the eve of Pentecost, and Tapia would much rather enjoy spending the great feastday in Santa Fe with his family. When Governor Peralta remained adamant, pointing out that the party could just as well hear Mass on Pentecost Sunday at one of the missions on the way, like San Juan, Tapia thoughtlessly went to see if Fray Ysidro might not change the lord governor's mind.

Immediately the father commissary got on his high horse—oblivious of the fact that St. Francis had emphatically forbidden his friars to ride on horseback in the spiritual as well as in the physical sense. Cunningly holding his peace for the time being, he later "chanced" to meet Tapia and his companions on their way to Taos, and gruffly ordered them to turn back to Santa Fe under threats of excommunication. On his return to the villa he proceeded to draw up a formal Inquisition case of contumacy against Peralta. Here is where Captain Romero began going back and forth between the palace and the Franciscan *convento* or friary, trying to extricate his brother-in-law and his son-in-law from the fracas; he likewise wanted to break the impasse between his civil and ecclesiastical superiors while saving face for both of them. However, matters had gone too far by now, and they were worsened by personal insults relayed through messengers across the intervening plaza or, with deadlier effect, by being dropped purposely in the presence of gossips. And now Fray Ysidro had called in all the missionaries from the pueblos closest to the villa, hence the emergency meeting called by the lord governor.

There had to be an explosion, and Luisa Robledo unwittingly lighted the fuse.

While Fray Ysidro's Mass had been going on in the hushed presence of Luisa and her terrified female companions, Don Pedro de Peralta, lord governor and captain-general of the kingdom, finished his conference at the palace with dispatch and then, lackey-ed by a group of armed followers, marched grimly across the plaza to the friary adjoining the church. He wore a shiny breastplate over his slashed satin doublet, and carried a small pistol stuck in his sash besides the larger-barreled one in his hand. Pushing through the entrance hall into the cloister yard, his party came face to face with the father guardian, who had just been telling his brethren that he felt like going over to the palace compound and felling the lord governor's prized bison heifers with a machete, just for spite. The three other friars, standing by the library door, looked scared, fearing that Peralta had caught this remark. But Don Pedro politely doffed his large plumed hat and requested to see the father commissary. The father guardian sullenly replied that Fray Ysidro was still saying Mass in the church, but then backed into the library door and shouted that the lord governor requested an audience.

Promptly Fray Ysidro filled the doorway. Still fuming from the affair inside the church, he brusquely asked Peralta his business in coming. His lordship merely wanted to know, in person, why and to what end so many friars were gathered in the capital, mumbling something else about excommunications and the rights of the representatives of the Crown. He spoke in a reserved man-ner, although his eyes and ears sharpened like a lynx's when he notice that the father guardian, muttering something about killing a dog, had gone inside and promptly returned with a stout walk-ing cane in his hand. Dog, eh? Swearing to Heaven that he him-self would hugely enjoy blasting off a friar's crown, Don Pedro raised and cocked his big pistol, ordering his men to search the convent for weapons. The men hesitated when Fray Ysidro threaten-ed them with automatic excommunication. But they proceeded to follow their master's orders when the pistol barrel switched over to them with a more ominous physical threat. No arms were found inside, however.

Meanwhile, sharp words kept on spitting back and forth be-tween the lord governor and the father commissary, until Fray Ysidro grabbed the heavy cane from the father guardian and raised it to strike Peralta. One soldier grasped Fray Ysidro's arm while others grappled with Don Pedro to prevent his lordship from committing a double sacrilege which could have far-reaching con-sequences for all those present. Killing a churchman, and on hallow-ed ground, could mean years of imprisonment in the far City of Mexico while being tried by the Inquisition, and then death if not permanent exile. By this time, too, another of the friars had come out brandishing a hefty bassoon from the choir. The pistol went off in the general scuffle, and an innocent bystander slipped with a groan onto the cloister rosebeds. One of the soldiers also let out a surprised scream of pain. Everything ceased immediately.

The innocent victim was the good laybrother, Fray Gerónimo de Pedraza—apothecary, physician, and nurse to the entire villa —whom everybody loved for his guilelessness and charity, and whose only crime, or misfortune, was to be present at the affair. Fortunately it was not a mortal wound. The lord governor's party left, probing the nether sides of one of their comrades where he had received a generous sprinkle of the grapeshot, while the friars at-tended to their wounded brother. But Fray Ysidro could not help overhearing the injured soldier's seething curses aimed at him in a strong blend of Spanish and Flemish, for the armorer Gaspar Pérez was a native of the Netherlands. Despite his being Captain Romero's new son-in-law, Fray Ysidro refused to grant him par-don and absolution later on when, only temporarily as it turned out, he did absolve Governor Peralta and the others from censure.

(Gómez Robledo was quick to notice how his sick niece's little features flinched whenever the story dwelt particularly on Fray Ysidro, as well as the nameless friar guardian. He would then explain to her that these men were glaring exceptions to the general rule. During the past fifty years all of Fray Ysidro's successors as superiors of the custody had been good priests and gentlemen, although they had their troubles with a few really bad governors. The rest of the friars had been fine men, although a few whom he knew personally did have a temper. A half dozen fathers in their lonely mission outposts had lived and died in the odor of advanced personal sanctity, he further added, while some other blessed ones had won the palm of martyrdom. This always calmed the sick girl, and Maria was grateful for her cousin's spontaneous explanation. At the same time Maria's inner eyes returned to contemplate Luisa Robledo. She must have been a most wonderful woman indeed —a grand old girl, as Cousin Francisco put it. And she could understand perfectly well why Aunt Ana never told her this story, for Luisa's screaming in church was not ladylike. Besides, there was Aunt Ana's brother-in-law, Gaspar Pérez, the wounded cursing *flamenco*, whom Cousin Francisco said was also suspected of being a heretic because he was from the Low Countries. And then there was Gaspar's only son, Diego Romero Pérez, who turned out to be worse yet. No wonder Aunt Ana was so silent about them. Not even gruff Cousin Francisco had dared to tell her about this son Diego.

(Maria learned about him by accident. Folks sometimes talk about certain matters when they think the children are fast asleep or beyond hearing distance. One very still night, when Maria could not sleep, although she was not feeling any pain, she listened intently to loud voices in the next room. Her parents and some visiting relatives were talking about this Diego, whom Maria never knew, for the Inquisition had sent for him years before she was born, and he never came back to his wife and people. Not only had Diego, a married man, fathered a child by a very young and innocent first cousin, also maltreated some good mission fathers and their poor Indians, and even joined the wild Indians of the plains in their false worship, but he had been found guilty of gross bestiality—whatever this last crime meant. It must have been some sort of witchcraft, Maria guessed, the kind by which Indian sorcerers were said to turn themselves into beasts, that the Inquisition took notice and hauled him off to New Spain, never to return.

(And poor Aunt Catalina de Zamora! She was Diego's forlorn wife. She was only Maria's number-two cousin, and only through marriage, but Maria had gotten used to regarding her as an aunt, for being so worn-out and old-looking. People called her *La Llorona*, because she was always crying. She howled at home, she wailed all the while she was visiting, she sobbed in church all during Mass. Her long furrowed face had a red and soggy look from it. But why shouldn't Aunt Catalina cry? Maria felt very sorry for her, knowing her husband's story, and because she realized that she was very lonely, having neither husband nor children. Aunt Ana Robledo would be horrified if she knew about her sick niece's eavesdropping, even if it was accidental—indeed, she would be more than annoyed if she ever learned how her son Francisco regaled Maria with other gossip, even if much less sordid, about the family.)

"My late husband, Francisco Gómez, was the best and noblest citizen this kingdom ever had." Thus Aunt Ana always began this phase of the family history. "He came from a family of Old Christians in Portugal. His parents died when he was a boy, and he was reared for a time by his eldest brother, who was a prominent priest of Lisbon. Then he was accepted as a page in the noble family of the Oñates. At the Court of Madrid he learned letters as well as the courteous manners of a gentleman, before coming to New Spain with our first governor's brother. It was my husband who escorted the great Governor Sotelo, who became my son Francisco's godfather in confirmation, all the way from the City of Mexico to Santa Fe; in this same party was Fray Alonso Benavides, who brought the statue of La Conquistadora to this parish church. And it was my husband, none else, who carried the banner of the Holy Office when those two gentlemen were solemnly installed as governor of the kingdom and custos of the custody. Later my husband and I initiated the society of La Conquistadora, and I have been the keeper of her wardrobe ever since. My son Francisco has been the society's majordomo or president ever since his wonderful father passed away. But my family's greatest distinction is that my husband was selected to be the lord governor and captain-general of the Kingdom of New Mexico."

Cousin Francisco laughed loud and long the first time Maria repeated Aunt Ana's boasts to him. "Yes, my proud little cousin, what my good mother told you is all very true. But what she left out is that my father (God keep him) never served as lord governor. You see, my own family and your father's have always held the high posts of the kingdom as residents of this villa of Santa Fe, but the real political power has lain in the hands of the Chávez, Baca, and Montoya people of the Rio Abajo, from San Felipe down to Isleta. We are not politicians; they live and breathe in-

trigue. Their children learn double-dealing better than their prayers. For as long as I can remember, they have been able to get
some of the mission fathers to take their side in many a controversy with the lord governors, as if the good of the missions were
their prime interest. Well, before Governor Flores died shortly
after his arrival here in the year 1641, he named my father to
succeed him until the King's next regular appointment came. But
those politicians stopped him from taking office. They went so
far as to denounce my father before the Inquisition, on false
charges that he was a Jewish *marrano* who secretly practiced the
Hebrew religion."

(Here Cousin Francisco would stop and look very grim and
serious, for a change. But after a while his eyes crinkled anew,
and his big frame began to shake with inner laughter.) "My
good old father was balding and was prone to head colds. He used
to wear a small black cap in the house, even at table, when he
also read to us from his books. For he did not wish his sons
and daughters to grow up to be ignorant jackasses, so he always
said, like the rest of the kingdom. And so he was accused of
being a *marrano*, or christianized Jew, who conducted secret
Jewish services for his family on Friday evenings. There was another
Jewish practice which we men of the family were accused of,
but you would not understand if I told you." (Here Cousin
Francisco would burst out with a loud guffaw.)

"Well, my father was never summoned by the Inquisition.
But I was, later. I spent three years down in the City of
Mexico answering those charges. It was not as bad as you might
imagine, for they kept me in their filthy jail only during those
periods when I had to appear before the tribunal. Between trials
I got acquainted with the beautiful city and its valley. And in my

appearances before the high tribunal I had a lot of fun answering those pompous judges who had no case to rest their chins on.

"They had to let me off, finally, and with honor. This all happened before you were born, Maria mine, and so it is all forgotten by now. I can imagine that our Rio Abajo politicians would prefer to forget it.

"As for your Aunt Ana being so ladylike—ay, she is a hard chip off her mother Luisa Robledo. One time a rich captain donated a lovely cream-colored mule to the society of La Conquistadora. The beast was to be sold to the highest bidder, and the proceeds used to buy brocades in New Spain for the Lady's mantles, or maybe for a new crown. But Governor Mendizábal appropriated the animal for his own use. Then you should have seen how my gentle little mother Ana made that governor give back the mule. Ay, the language that she used on him would have made a mule-driver proud. And sometime after that, Governor Peñalosa fared worse at her hands. Mother was visiting at the palace one day, when Peñalosa called her to one side and made a shameful proposition concerning herself and her youngest daughter, my sister Anamaria. Mother practically gouged out that fellow's eyes!"

(While Cousin Francisco slapped his thigh and chuckled merrily on, Maria's thoughts went back again to Aunt Ana and her mother Luisa. She thought more of them now than ever before. It was understandable why a woman would not care to mention certain things, of course, and especially those matters that had to do with the Inquisition. Yet, as to the possibility of Uncle Gómez having been a Jew, or the son of a converted Jew in Portugal, Maria herself began to wish that Uncle Gómez had been her own grandfather, as he was of her little Gómez Robledo cousins who sometimes came to play at her bedside. It was not only to inherit the same flaming red hair that they had, and their greenish blue eyes, although she herself was not ashamed of her black Romero hair and the darker Archuleta complexion derived from her mother Josefa, but most especially to have some of that blood which ran through the veins of the Savior and His Mother. At this thought, it looked to Maria as though the little Lady in her niche quivered with pleasant assurance and then drew closer to her tear-blurred eyes.)

But the high sheriff himself, the *sargento mayor* (or major) Bartolomé Romero, just because he was Maria Romero's own father, and such a dear father, was the one who showered the most happiness all about her room and in her very heart. He did not have to say anything either, no heroic family tales, to make his crippled daughter's aches ebb fast away, or at least it seemed that way. When he did speak of affairs outside, it was about things connected with his office as high sheriff. Maria felt that he told them to her because no one else would listen with so much interest, or understand—except men like Father Bernal of Galisteo. Moreover, she wanted to hear about them because they had to do with what Father Bernal had hinted as being an intimate part of her sufferings.

Not that Bartolomé Romero was gloomy, like Josefa de Archuleta. Unlike his wife, he wore the warmest of smiles when he came in and embraced his invalid daughter. While others might complain about the severe drought of several years which was working havoc among the colonists and the mission Indians, he told Maria how wonderful the sierras looked in the summer or winter sun. In spring he brought Maria slips of willow from the villa's stream with their tiny kittens clinging all along their edges. In summer there were bunches of purple verbena and red pent-stemons from the juniper hills on the way to Tesuque. This past harvest time, he brought her an aspen branch tinkling noiselessly with perfectly round golden leaves, like coins—her father saying it was a money tree with genuine gold *reales* from the King's mint in Spain.

Maria's only regret was that Bartolomé was all too often away from home, even though she was so proud of the fact that he was a most important official of the entire kingdom. This took him to the far ends of it, and it was from his descriptions that she could reconstruct the varied landscapes of mountain, plain, and desert, as also the many mission churches of the pueblos. Moreover, the family's lands and herds were extensive. He had to see to the proper care of the crops from spring to harvest, and to the wel-fare of his livestock all the year around. Still more, he had to inspect and alert the Indian warriors in one pueblo whenever there were rumors of a raid by the gentile Indians of the plains, especially the Apaches, who grew more dangerous every year because they now had many horses and rode them like the wind. The villa of Santa Fe was said to be secure from such attacks because of its location, and the presidio, but the far-flung Indian missions and the people of the open Spanish haciendas, some not too distant from the villa, had been losing not only horses but precious human lives as well.

Above all, the post of *alguacil mayor* was one of deep religious and civil responsibility, if one of supreme distinction. His duty it was to make personal arrests at the request of the lord governor or of the father custos, depending on whether the crime was committed against the kingdom or the custody. Bartolomé would laugh quietly whenever Maria asked him if he had arrested any-body of late, always bending down to kiss her and saying that she was his only prisoner, one whom he never would release. Then he would explain how there were not so many arrests to be made as in former times. In the very old days, when his father and grandfather served as high sheriffs, the lord governor and the father custos were often at loggerheads. One day the sheriff was arresting the lord governor's men at the demand of the father su-perior, and next day he was apprehending those who were siding with the friars in the current controversy. This was because a few bad governors, not all the governors were bad by any means, sent their henchmen to despoil the mission Indians of their maize or the fine cotton sheets they wove, or else made them work for nothing. These coarse individuals said very insulting words to the mission fathers when they defended their Indians; then the fathers got raving mad at the bad words, and so began excommunicating their foes and calling loudly for the high sheriff. In his grand-father's day, the father superior, whose name was Fray Ysidro, took the lord governor's chair from its place of honor near the altar of the parish church and tossed it out on the plaza. That was sometime before Governor Peralta accidentally shot the good phy-sician, Fray Gerónimo, and also Uncle Gaspar Pérez, the Flemish husband of Aunt Maria Romero.

(Little Maria could not help thinking about Gaspar's son Diego, the black sheep of the Romero family who was arrested by the In-quisition and never returned. She wondered who had made that arrest, but dared not ask her father, who would be most displeased to learn about her eavesdropping, even if it was not on pur-pose, or almost so.)

Things must have been most difficult in those days, her father continued, especially for the poor sheriff caught in-between the authorities and his close relatives. But that was all over now, except for a few hardheads and ne'er-do-wells who were still voicing their petty grievances against the friars. But these, like good Father Bernal, did not blast back scandalously like Fray Ysidro. While most of the mission fathers were not altogether perfect, as what poor humans are, there had been wonderful friars, like Father Letrado who was martyred at Zuñi in the days of his father Bartolomé, who led an expedition to avenge his death. There were Fathers Zárate and Llana who had labored quietly and meekly for years in the loneliest of the missions, and with such personal goodness that both the good Indians and the Spaniards regarded them as saints in Heaven. And there was Father Bernardo de Marta, who had worked devotedly for over twenty-five years in the isolated mission of Zia; although dead for many years now, the people still prayed to him because he had lived so holily that his Indians claimed that he had worked miracles in their behalf. This is why the Zias had not had *estufas* for a long time. Even today, there was Father Bernal of Galisteo, a wonderful man. And in the Moqui pueblo of Xongopavi there was a Father Trujillo, whom the friars themselves regarded as a living saint.

His daughter's peculiar interest in the *estufas* and *cachinas* prodded Romero into explaining the touchy matter of those ceremonial chambers and the masked dances, which were the underlying cause for most major quarrels of the past. From the beginning, the friars had wanted the *estufas* destroyed, and the *cachinas* done away with. Otherwise, the pueblo Indians would never become true Christians. For in these chambers the *caciques* and the other "old men," the heads of the different clans and secret societies, worshipped and con-

From Toledo

sulted their false gods. These were tiny animal fetishes of stone and turquoise to which they set up prayersticks adorned with turkey feathers. Or they sprinkled the meal or the pollen of maize on them, as the priests of Holy Church used holy water. Here they also taught their young men the heathen beliefs and chants of their fore-fathers. The *cachina* dances were a form of worship to these gods and to the scalps of their enemies, and they usually ended in ob-scene spectacles in which the clowns or *coxares* made the people take part.

As the best example of this, Bartolomé Romero liked to re-count a vivid experience related to him by his own grandfather. In the year 1626, the first Bartolomé surprised the south Tiguas of Alameda running riot inside their mission church—*"faciendo sus mitotes"* or doing their shenanigans, as his grandfather used to put it. The pueblo's *cacique* perched on the pulpit was scream-ing and working himself into a trance, in order to contact the other-world spirits, while the painted naked *cachina* dancers—a very big mulatto among them—were trying to catch his frenzy. Shocked beyond measure, Captain Romero pulled the leader from the pulpit and beat him senseless, while his men drove the sacrilegious crowd with their whips and swords out of the holy place.

(*Cachina* sounded so much like the Spanish word for "sow," that Maria almost visualized the dancers wallowing like hogs in a sty. Then the thought of those false gods, to which the dances were dedicated, prompted her to ask her father about that mys-terious gigantic black god of Po-he-yemu. Did not the Indians say that he was a mighty guardian spirit of their customs, and that he kept watch over all hearts with his big yellow eyes?).

Bartolomé would wave his arms with unbelief. He said it was

only a fairy tale. The Mexican Indians whom the earliest Spaniards left among the pueblos had taught them their own ancient myth about their hero-god Huitzilopochtli, founder of the City of Mexico. These pueblo Indians then confused him with the Emperor Moctezuma—whom they called Po-he-yemu in their own manner of speaking. And they further claimed that he dwelt by the blue mountain lake near the pueblo of Taos. Such an unreal being posed no problem for the authorities—it was the underground temples and the secret dances that were the high sheriff's headache.

In order to spite the fathers for previous spats, Maria's father went on, some Spanish governors and bad elements among the lesser officials allowed the Indians to keep their *estufas* and secret dances. They even advised them to disobey the fathers when the bell rang for Mass or for the catechism. Sometimes the *caciques* and *principales* paid these officials with buckskins and hides of bison, or sacks of *piñon*. By now the mission Indians had become accustomed to keeping their pagan worship while they considered themselves Christians at the same time. Of course, there were many pueblo Indians who were genuine Catholics and refused to take part in all these pagan practices. Now, it was his own bounden duty as high sheriff to see that these practices were suppressed, and many of the fathers were continually urging him to do it. He hated to act, however, not because he was afraid of doing the right thing, or that he feared for his life, but because each time he should raze an *estufa* or break up a *cachina*, the medicinemen might vent their wrath upon the poor defenseless missionary in each pueblo.

(This was the only time that Maria ever noticed a shadow cross her father's unusually blue eyes, such beautiful eyes which Aunt

From Toledo

Ana said came from the Robledos, together with his fair skin, while his jet-black hair came from the Romero side. And then kindly Father Bernal's moist hazel eyes came up, too, begging Maria to offer up her pains in expiation for the sins of the kingdom. But which, exactly, were the sins of the kingdom? Was it the struggle of the *caciques* of the pueblos to keep their own pagan worship? Or could it be the superstitions and attempts at witchery which some of the colonists had picked up from their Indian neighbors, like that Griego woman who poisoned Grandmother Granillo? Was it the arrogance of a man like Fray Ysidro, or the dishonest arbitrary ways of a few governors like Mendizábal and Peñalosa? Maybe it was the lying intrigues of the politicians of the Rio Abajo—or else the heinous things done by men like Diego Romero Pérez?)

* *   * *   * *   * *   * *   * *   * *

Poor Maria Romero lay moaning all alone, suddenly grown hot all over her emaciated little body. Her bed was now a clammy thing of torture, although this very morning Josefa de Archuleta had tenderly bathed her child and soothed her bedsores with the cooling salve of fragrant herbs. She had also freshened up the bed with smooth clean sheets, and put a crisp laundered gown on the sick girl, before going out to do her other household chores. But the burning fever and unbearable pains began soon after she left.

The night before had been one of those familiar sleepless ones, full of fearsome noises which Maria had drowned out with the storytelling voices of Aunt Ana and Cousin Francisco and her own beloved father. The long siege of mental pictures all through the night had left her head feeling as though it were swollen from within; but now the balls of her eyes, instead of giving in to tired slumber as happened after other sleepless nights, wanted to pop out of her face. As the fever mounted, the pain grew heavier and heavier upon all her bones. Maria had never felt such excruciating aches as now, especially all over and through her little chest, and her heart, which now began to pound, pound, pound, like a frightened child wanting to be let out of a locked closet.

Maria now knew for sure that she was about to die. Her soul was begging for release, as folks put it. It was the hour which Father Bernal had pronounced for her. "For the sins of the kingdom, for the sins of the kingdom." Now was the time to make the final offering of her agony to the good God Who was in Heaven. There she would soon see Him face to face, and also that Lady who had filled the few pain-racked years of her earthly life with the only joys she ever knew.

Maria made one last grim effort to fix her gaze upon the wall opposite, to take one last look at the little vested figure in her niche. To her joyful amazement, she saw the little Lady growing larger and larger, and moving toward her as if muffled in rainbows. Maria could feel the joy of this surprise because her pain melted fast away as the Lady came closer, shimmering like a star of sparkling blue and pink lights in the wet window of her tears. This, Maria was sure, was the other side of death, the very portal of Heaven.

And then Maria heard the Lady speaking loud and clear.

"*Niña,*" she said. "My darling child. You are not going to die, yet. Get up, my dear Maria. You are now well. Get up and tell the people that the kingdom and custody will soon be destroyed. It is because the colonists all these years have shown so little respect for their priests, and thus spoiled the conversion of the native Indians. Do not worry, child, for when the people see you perfectly healed, they will be convinced that what I am telling you is true. You must also beg them to make amends for their sins and faults, if they themselves wish to escape the punishment that is coming for sure."

Out on the plaza, returning home from some errand, Josefa de Archuleta stopped short, herself now paralyzed for the moment, as soon as she saw her crippled daughter walking out the door unaided and perfectly steady, in fact, graceful in her walk. Maria was joyously calling her name and Ana Robledo's. The girl's beaming face and clear ringing voice were no less a marvel than the fact of her walking unassisted, of walking at all. Then came the strong and tight embrace of mother and daughter which left no doubt—*Nuestra Señora del Sagrario* had indeed cured little Maria Romero at last, and by a sudden miracle such as one reads in the lives of the saints.

This was the cry which sped through the villa after Josefa had recovered her wits and listened to the girl's explanation, after Aunt Ana came rushing from her house, and also the friars from the parish church, when Maria was made to repeat what the Lady had said to her, again and again. The plaza was soon filled with the people of the villa, and from Analco across the little river. While the fathers let out sonorous strophes of praise and admiration for all to hear, the townsfolk listened in quiet awe. They tended rather to silence in the face of such a momentous happening, pondering over the terrifying portent of the message. The miracle of the cure was all too obvious, and therefore the message had to be true. Those individuals who had prepared complaints to mail to the City of Mexico when the next supply train arrived, lost no time running home to burn up the letters. Certain officials went through the governmental archive in the palace to destroy petitions for lawsuits which they had filed therein. The ordinary innocent folk struck their breasts for any untoward thought they might have entertained.

The next morning the parish church of the villa was packed for a solemn Mass in which a stirring sermon was preached. Little Maria, glowing with humble joy as well as her newly found health, sat up front in a place of honor next to the lord governor's throne. On the high altar itself, the little Lady from Toledo shared the honors with the patronal image of La Conquistadora.

By this time the marvelous news had spread out from the capital of the kingdom in every direction. It flew from nearby hacienda to nearby pueblo mission, from further pueblo mission to the furthest hacienda, up to the high valleys of Taos and Picuris and down the winding course of the Rio del Norte to the lowlands of Socorro and Senecú. It breezed from mouth to mouth, or in notes carried by fleet Indian runners, eastward to the Pecos country and also west to Zia and Jémez, thence to Acoma and faraway Zuñi—and from Zuñi northwestward to the little mission of San Bartolomé on the lofty cliff pueblo of Xongopavi.

PART TWO:

THE PADRE AND THE SLAVE

THE PADRE AND THE SLAVE

1. THE LONG ROAD OF FATHER TRUJILLO

To an eagle straying far aloft from the Kaibab forests over the great cliff-strewn desert of the Moqui, the lofty promontories of Xongopavi and her four sister pueblos might look like petrified fronds of some giant fern lying dead for ages on a dried lake bottom. To puny earthbound creatures like the Moqui people, who called themselves the *hopi*, the peaceful, the several irregular projections looked more like huge individual tables of rock set at a good distance from each other; on each of them their forefathers had long ago built their stone and mud towns as perfect refuges from any foe. While Spanish soldiers had been allowed to visit these sky villages, the actual storming of them had not been tested. A nominal conquest had been made by unarmed friars of St. Francis when one of them temporarily awed the *caciques* by restoring the sight of a boy born blind; this one conquest was marked by a mission church on Xongopavi and three of the other pueblos.

To old Fray José de Trujillo, though without the least tinge of nostaglia, all of these mesas were also like castles in Spain, those stark medieval ruins capping bare upsurging hills in arid sections of extreme western Castile, even if not near so tall as these incredible natural fortresses bathed in eternal sun and silence. Sometimes, to relieve the monotony, Father Trujillo played over the scene with his eyes, turning the desert below a marine blue like South Sea water, the distant cliffs a lush green like some craggy volcanic islands in the tropics. His own cliff of Xongopavi became an immense galleon from whose tall tilted forward deck he surveyed both the present scene and the lengthy panorama of his varied life. And as a sea-voyager scans the horizon for signs of human contact, he examined the eastern edges for a tiny bit of motion, perhaps a band of soldiers who had wandered far west from Santa Fe, or maybe the friar of Zuñi, his closest neighbor, coming over for their mutual confessions and a day or two of religious chit-chat.

Such signs were few and far between, however, and Father Trujillo, habitually left in peace by his overly peaceful flock, was forced to vary his anachoritic fare of prayers by gathering about him his life-long dreams and recollections. Or else he wrote let- ters, to be mailed God knew when, to his brethren at El Convento Grande in the City of Mexico.

When young José de Trujillo embarked for the Indies at the port of Cádiz, his birthplace, he had no fixed goal in mind like the rest of his fellow voyagers. These consisted of a goodly number of soldiers of fortune, merchants, government officials, and a dozen Franciscans who had arrived from La Rábida before the ship raised anchor. All he knew for the present was what the ship's master had told him.

An uncle, whom he barely remembered, and who had developed a prosperous tradesman's house at Puebla de los Angeles in New Spain, had paid the captain to find this nephew of his and bring him back to Puebla on the return voyage. José understood that his uncle had no children, and that he was to learn his merchandizing business, evidently to inherit it some day. If he were not so poor, and if his parents had not already died, he might not have accepted the offer. Trading had never appealed to him, although he had a sharp mind, could read very well, and wrote a very handsome script. Or so he was told whenever he wrote letters for people to relatives in the New World. If he got tired of making bills of lading for his uncle, he could very well find employment as a private scrivener, perhaps even as the lord viceroy's secretary.

It bothered him, this lack of a definite purpose in life. Having no taste at all for violence and danger, he held himself aloof from the soldiers and other adventurers who talked about nothing else but rich mines and plunder on the frontiers of New Spain. He preferred the company of the friars on board, but only because he had always been a pious lad by nature, not from any appeal their way of life had for him. Yet, to be a mere merchant, no matter how prosperous, or even the privy secretary of some great personage, this was not enough. Something was missing.

His uncle turned out to be a very rich man, wealthier than he had expected, and who received José like a doting father. Instead of introducing the youth to his business affairs right away, he sent him to pursue further studies in "Grammar and Philosophy," to make him a well-rounded gentleman, as his uncle put it. But neither these studies nor the excitements provided by the bustling activities in this strange new land, nor even the exotic beauties of a country so different from the drab landscape near Cádiz, could keep José from slipping into moods of despondency—until the answer came one night, startlingly sudden like a shot, and as clear and as unmistakeable as if some twigs by his window had dropped on the sill and spelled out a certain word.

Early next morning, José knocked at the friary of Our Lady of the Angels in Puebla, and requested to be given the humble livery of St. Francis. The novice master, Fray Francisco de Rondero, almost burst out laughing when the young man revealed his reason for wanting to become a Franciscan. His preceding answers and his references had so far been of the very best, as was his personal appearance. The rather slight body looked strong and healthy enough, while the angular intelligent countenance, a little dark but brightened by the candid black eyes, was almost handsome. The youth's entire presence radiated an inner innocence seldom seen in young Spaniards after a short stay in the Indies. Here, no doubt, was an excellent candidate for the Order.

But this! The laughter never started from the priest's ample middle, for Father Rondero suddenly recalled that only the evening before he had preached a sermon on the life of the greatly beloved St. Anthony of Padua. He had made much of the fact that Anthony had become a Franciscan with the single idea of becoming a martyr. And now this personable young man before him had exactly the same notion. Had young Trujillo heard the sermon perhaps? No, he had not. Last night it had come to him, sharp and clear, from out the starry heavens, said José with utter guilelessness.

And so, on September the thirtieth, of the year 1633, José de

From Toledo

Trujillo received the rough blue garb of the Franciscans of the province of the Holy Gospel, while his disappointed but piously resigned uncle looked on as his *padrino* with tears in his kindly eyes.

José soon learned why the new habit he received was of a blue wool serge instead of the grey to which he had been used to seeing back at La Rábida. He wondered if it had anything to do with the Blessed Virgin Mary, since Spanish priests wore blue silk vestments for Masses in honor of the Immaculate Conception. Father Rondero said his guess was correct. Quite a few years ago the Franciscans of Spain had assumed an extra vow to defend and promote the doctrine of the Immaculate Conception; and less than twenty years ago, the friars in the custody of New Mexico had reported that a nun in blue had been appearing among the pagan wild tribes of that distant region, teaching them the doctrines of the Church. The famed Father Alonso Benavides had not only heard those Indians describe the nun and her garb, but he had also heard Mother Maria de Agreda tell him personally that she had been transported several times, in the wink of an eye, all the way from her convent in Spain to those wilderness regions. She belonged to the Conceptionist Nuns, a Spanish branch of the Second Order of St. Francis; the members of this community wore a blue mantle as a sign of their particular devotion to the Immaculate Conception. All this, and the fact that bright and fast aniline dyes had been arriving from the Philippines missions at this time, had prompted the friars of the Holy Gospel to begin dyeing their habits blue. The practice pleased the new friar, for more reasons than he could right then explain.

During the year-long novititate, Fray José de Trujillo not only absorbed the lore and spirit of the Franciscan life, to the great satisfaction of Father Rondero, but he displayed an unusual grasp of certain fundamentals underlying the vows he was to make, especially with what concerned a perfect obedience without which convent life can be a painful experience, if not a mockery. Yet, the wise novice master, a sensible man at bottom, privately advised him not to lose sight of the strange desire that had led him to the cloister. Martyrdom in itself was a laudable goal, whether it came or not, if sought within the frame of obedience. St. Anthony of Padua had proved it; he never attained this prime desire, yet it was because of this that he had excelled in other pursuits which Providence, through obedience, had laid out for him.

In pondering over these matters, the young novice also had occasion to put together the various factors which had helped to crystallize this certain goal so mysteriously in his heart.

A major topic of conversation in New Spain, at the time José arrived in Puebla, was the heroic martyrdom of several missionaries in the frontier posts of the fast-expanding Spanish Empire in America and in the Orient. It was something altogether new and fresh in a period when the talk about new discoveries and of fabled kingdoms, though still going strong, had grown stale for lack of variety. Dying for the Faith—a sure gauge of eternal salvation attained without passing through the refining crucible of Purgatory—profoundly impressed the layman on the streets and in the taverns as much as it did the friar in his convent. While they might shudder with understandable diffidence at having to suffer torture onto death as witnesses for Christ, they reveled in the thought of having once known, in the flesh, a person who now saw Christ face to face following a bloody heroic ordeal. Many had heard the martyr preach before he left for distant missions; others had confessed their sins to him, and treasured some bit of sage advice if not a palpable token, like a medal or a rosary.

There had been no such matyrdoms in the conquest of Mexico or in the decades that followed, in spite of the bitterness engendered among the natives by the rapacity of Cortés' men and some of their successors. The Tlascalans had been friendly allies and then eager converts from the start, a fact which was illustrated by the faith of the natives in and around Puebla; in fact, it was a practice with the mission friars to take groups of them to use as a seed of Faith by planting them among the savage northern tribes which they set out to civilize. The brutal blow of the conquest throughout the valley of Mexico and its environs had been softened with the arrival of the famed Franciscan "twelve apostles," whose hands the iron Conquerer himself had knelt down to kiss before the eyes of the beaten Aztecs, and these had henceforth responded amazingly to their goodness.

And a few years after that, these same Aztecs had been visited from on high with the favors and the very portrait of the Queen of Heaven, tendered through the humble Juan Diego, one of their own. The shrine which treasured the miraculous picture of their very own Lady of Guadalupe in Tepeyac also recalled the fond memory of their beloved protector, Fray Juan de Zumárraga, the first bishop and archbishop of Mexico. As a consequence, there had not been any violent deaths of missionaries in the otherwise colorful period of the conquest and the years following.

It is true that some friars had been killed by the fierce Chichimecas in the north frontier shortly after the year 1540. And much further north, around the same time, Fray Juan de Padilla and Fray Luis de Ubeda had died for the Faith in the still mysterious land of "the new Mexico," shortly after Don Francisco Vásquez de Coronado had led a memorable expedition thither, almost a century ago. But the details of these two friars' heroism were lost. Their contemporaries had been too busy pressing forward in their overwhelming mission enterprises to pause and properly record the testimonies of witnesses. When they thought of it decades later, it was too late. Hence, only slim and cloudy legends remained like a faint halo around their hallowed names.

But what José de Trujillo had heard in his uncle's stores and warehouses, in the classrooms, in the open market square of Puebla, let alone the various pulpits, was something which had happened within the memory of many of his new fellow citizens. There were some old people who actually remembered Fray Pedro Bautista, or else one or more of his companions, all of whom were crucified in Japan in 1597. Mostly, these admiring folk liked to dwell longer on one of these companions of the Blessed Pedro Bautista. He was the young Fray Felipe de la Casa y Martínez, known in the Franciscan Order as Fray Felipe de Jesús. Born of well-to-do parents in the City of Mexico—a gay blade and a prankster according to local tradition—Felipe had entered the novitiate, only to be bored soon after with convent routine. Young Martínez then took off for the Philippines, spurred by wild tales of adventure brought back by sailors and soldiers returning on galleons that plied the South Sea lanes between Acapulco and Manila. In Manila, these people said, Felipe led a riotous life before becoming serious again and re-entering the Order in that city. (To José de Trujillo, Felipe's carousing seemed very much exaggerated, since the ocean voyage itself took months, and Felipe sought re-admittance well within the twelve-month since he left the novitiate in the City of Mexico.)

Anyhow, Fray Felipe persevered this time, prayed and studied

From Toledo

hard for four years, and received the minor sacred orders from the bishop of Manila. Unfortunately, the bishop died before Fray Felipe de Jesús could receive the major orders culminating in the priesthood. For this reason he was sent back to the City of Mexico for ordination. (Again, Trujillo took it with a grain of salt when people said that Fray Felipe really was sent back to New Spain for ordination because his parents happened to be wealthy and influential. Of course, it could have been so.)

The galleon on which Felipe set sail from Manila was caught by a typhoon and blown to the coast of Japan. There he found temporary refuge in a small Franciscan community headed by Fray Pedro Bautista. It so happened that a few weeks later the Japanese Emperor was prevailed upon by his advisers to do away with the Christians, and he had them all arrested and crucified. The very first one to be nailed to a cross at Nagasaki, and then spitted to it with a lance, was none other than Fray Felipe de Jesús.

Thus on February the fifth, 1597, the wild young one of the City of Mexico became the very first Christian martyr of Japan. Thirty years later, in 1627, these martyrs, Spaniards and native Japanese, were beatified by his Holiness the Pope. This provided the City of Mexico with an occasion for a most especial kind of celebration, since the friar martyrs had walked its streets and breathed its atmosphere at various times, but most especially because one of them was a native son. In the mammoth procession to the cathedral, Blessed Felipe's own mother walked proudly between their lordships, the archbishop and the viceroy. A similar celebration was observed every year thereafter in Fray Felipe's native city.

There were other such martyrs in Japan, beheaded and burned

in very recent years. Several of them had acquaintances and relatives in the Indies. One of these, the laybrother Fray Bartolomé Laurel, was likewise a native of New Spain; he had been beheaded by the Japanese only seven years before, in 1627. A goldsmith in Puebla had told young Trujillo that he had known Brother Bartolomé since they were boys, and was certain that this martyr, too, would be beatified someday like the Blessed Felipe. And José recalled that the man had said it with great feeling, proud and profoundly devout at the same time.

Others spoke of some very recent martyrs in that far northern region, of which Friars Padilla and Ubeda were remembered as misty pioneers. There was a well-established Spanish colony in that area, called the Kingdom of New Mexico. Many Franciscan missionaries were laboring in its many isolated Indian missions which comprised the Custody of the Conversion of St Paul. Not quite three years before, in 1630, the Indians of the pueblo of Zuñi had killed Fray Francisco Letrado and Fray Martín de Arvide, and the following year those of the pueblo of Taos murdered Fray Pedro de Miranda. All three were known personally to many people in Puebla de los Angeles.

By reflecting on these many martydroms of his day, which kept coming up frequently in cloister conversations, as well as in the many pious lectures of Father Rondero, Novice Trujillo soon solved the mystery of the sudden enlightenment which had led him into the Order. He, too, wanted to be a martyr like Martínez and Laurel in the Far East. It further explained the strange delight he had felt on learning why his New World brethren dyed their habits blue, tenuous as was the connection with the aniline dyes from the Orient. But he gave most of the credit to the Blessed Felipe de Jesús—the picture of the martyr's own mother walking in the beatification procession between the lord archbishop and the lord viceroy always returned to his mind. He would ask to be sent to Japan on the happy longed-for day of his ordination.

The twelvemonth-long novitiate ended, Fray José de Trujillo professed his solemn vows on the first day of October, 1634. He was then twenty-four years of age. Right away he was dispatched to San Francisco del Convento Grande in the City of Mexico for his course in philosophy and theology. Here his intimate contact with the birthplace of the Blessed Felipe and the more recent martyr, Brother Laurel, fanned his secret resolve to a white heat during the four years of concentrated study. He also felt his natural talents greatly sharpened and enlightened by his secret flame.

Once, for a brief spell, he thought that he might ask to be assigned to the missions of New Mexico, for recently a Fray Francisco de Porras, who had gained entrance into the unfriendly Moqui pueblos by miraculously giving sight to a boy born blind, was poisoned afterward by the envious witchdoctors of the pueblo of Aguátubi. It was the same year in which Fray José had received his call to martyrdom, and the garb of St. Francis. It could be a sign that he, too, should find his goal upon those high rock villages of Moqui. But the picture of Blessed Felipe de Jesús and Japan was too deeply engraved in his soul to be forgotten for long. He would go to the Orient.

In his ardent application to duty, however, in the chapel choir as well as in the lecture hall, Fray José had failed to notice, or even suspect, the ever-growing admiration for him in the eyes of his superiors and lectors. Shortly after his ordination in 1638, on the occasion of his maiden sermon, he was named conventual preacher of El Convento Grande, a title coveted by most, and granted only to a select few, after years of proven excellence in preaching. A canon of the cathedral of Mexico who heard him— Don Juan de Arze also held the chair of Sacred Scripture at the Royal University and, like most secular clergy of his day, subscribed to the opinion that the friars should be neither seen nor heard (*zapatero a tu zapato, fraile a tu convento*)—declared with utter amazement that he had never witnessed such a command of Holy Writ in all his thirty years of study and teaching. The friars themselves recalled a similar incident in the life of St. Anthony of Padua. Foiled in his attempt to encounter martyrdom in Morocco, the unknown Anthony was serving obscurely in an Italian friary when he was called upon to supply for a famous preacher who had failed to arrive; the assembly before him was one of high prelates and doctors of theology and Scripture. Needless to say, Anthony astounded them all. So it was with young Father Trujillo.

He was appointed master of novices soon after, and for ten years he tried very hard to emulate the holy Doctor of Padua whom circumstances, and religious obedience, had forced on him for a model instead of the Protomartyr of Japan. Yet, because wise Father Rondero had said that he could keep his original desire and goal in mind—and perhaps Anthony had also, ever hoping to be slain by the Albigenses of Provence or those other heretics of Rimini by the Adriatic—Fray José de Trujillo kept on praying so much for that blessed consummation that in 1648, when a band of missionaries was about to depart for the Far East, he could not help asking his father provincial to let him accompany them. To his joyous surprise, he was told that he could go. He sailed from Acapulco shortly thereafter, already fourteen years a friar and ten years a priest. The palm of the Blessed Philip of Mexico and Nagasaki was now plainly in sight.

Religious travel orders, like military ones in every age, can be countermanded enroute by other major superiors, Fray José soon found out after docking in Manila. The superior of the missions in Luzón tersely told him that the present shipment of missionaries to Japan was immediately needed in these Philippine islands. His own assignment would be the isle of Calonga. Had Fray José not been accustomed to thinking about St. Anthony and Father Rondero, he would have rebelled then and there. But he also remembered that the Lord Himself had allowed a little complaint to escape His lips in the Garden of Olives, and so he went out to seek a bit of solace from someone who might understand.

In a nunnery of Manila there lived an old wrinkled mother superior who for many years enjoyed the reputation of a sage counsellor. Father Trujillo had heard of this Sor Juana de San Antonio before disembarking. She was held in highest esteem by tired missionaries in need of some motherly solace. If the spirit of perfect obedience forbade him to question the wisdom of his own male superiors, it surely did not curb him from unburdening his soul to someone so wise and holy, if only to relieve an internal pressure that might prove harmful eventually.

Mother Juana turned out to be more unbelievable than he had been led to expect. For, after listening patiently, and as if she knew his whole life before his words spilled out, she told him with calm assurance that he would never find the palm of martyrdom in Japan, even if he did get there. She began to look utterly ridiculous, in fact, when she said that he would someday reach his goal in the custody of New Mexico. Now, this was impossible. An assignment to the Orient was one of no return, except a dishonorable one. He did not have the faintest excuse, like the Blessed Philip's, to be sent back to New Spain—the only gate-way to the missions of New Mexico. Perhaps old age was affect-ing the judgment of Sor Juana de San Antonio. Precisely because of this, he gave the matter no further thought.

The mission of Calonga proved to be most interesting from the start. Father Trujillo loved the simple people. In his letters to El Convento Grande he described his many hardships due to a scarcity of supplies, his attempts at building churches with soggy palm logs and buggy thatches of *nipa*, but he wrote with a cheer-ful spirit. In one letter written from Terrenate, in June of 1656, after outlining the many inconveniences, he cheerfully comment-ed that God, "Who takes care of the little sparrows, will not forget those who want to serve Him." Reports also began reach-ing Manila that Father Trujillo had been performing little miracles for his flocks, as when he made a spring of pure sweet water burst out of the swampy ground by sheer force of praying and pounding on the salitric earth with his mission cross.

But knowledge of his intellectual gifts had also reached Manila from New Spain. He was drawn out of the mission field immedi-ately and assigned to the islands' capital for duties more com-mensurate with his learned qualifications. To Father Trujillo it was all the same now, since he was convinced that the door to martyrdom was closed to him forever.

It was almost ten years since he had embarked at Acapulco when orders came from El Convento Grande specifying his im-mediate return to the City of Mexico. His own father provincial needed his services at his own headquarters if he was not to be employed in mission work. But Father Trujillo's first thought was of a parallel in the life of blessed Felipe de Jesús—his ship might also be blown to the coast of Japan by a storm, and to martyrdom, in spite of old Mother Juana de San Antonio. The galleon, however, reached Acapulco after a long return voyage over a pacific South Sea. The great ocean was so calm all the way, the winds so mild, that the ship took much longer than its usual schedule.

There was a group of returning Jesuit missionaries aboard who later told some amazing stories about their lone Franciscan shipmate. They had been impressed at the very start when the ship's captain asked Fray José if he had forgotten to bring his luggage aboard, and the friar, pointing to his shabby habit and his dog-eared breviary, replied: "I have it all here with me." Later, during some very chilly days and nights on the high seas, one of the Jesuits had pressed on him a pair of thick socks to cover his bare feet; but Father Trujillo kept them tucked in his sleeve until he returned them unused when the cold spell was over. But the chief anecdote was one similar to the water miracle of Calonga which already had reached America. The ship's casks of drinking water were dangerously low, because of the extra long and slow voyage, when Father Trujillo assured the troubled crew and passengers that the casks were full to the brim. And so it turned out. The fact that these Jesuits related a miracle wrought by a friar was enough proof in New Spain to the incontestable truth of it.

On reaching El Convento Grande, which looked as immense as ever, and still warm with holy memories as on the day he had left it, Father Trujillo discovered the reason for his unexpected recall. The province of the Holy Gospel was re-founding the Friary of Recollection at San Cosme, and his provincial could think of no better man than Fray José to help in the enterprise. For this was a very especial kind of convent, an exclusive cloister for meditation where long-term missionaries, as well as city pastors and lectors, might retire voluntarily for stated periods, to chip off in silent seclusion the barnacles and rust of the world which willy-nilly had encrusted their souls during their apostolic work. The permanent staff had to be composed of friars of a certain calibre, and Father Trujillo had come to mind from the first.

To him it was like being master of novices all over again, as though his decade-long jaunt over the great ocean and the lush green islands had been but an overnight dream between his first residence at El Convento Grande and now the cloisters of San Cosme. The illusion grew so much stronger when, six years after San Cosme was founded anew, the novitiate was transferred thither from El Convento Grande, and he became guardian of both the recollection section and the novitiate. This was in 1667, when he was fifty-seven years old, and when he thought less and less of Japan and her Blessed Felipe. He hardly ever thought of old Mother Juana of Manila. And in the meantime little stories about him seeped out of San Cosme to make the rounds of the religious refectories as well as the secular taverns of the City of Mexico.

One of them concerned a little white dove which Father Trujillo kept for a pet, the same dove that was set loose in the church every Pentecost Sunday at the intoning of the *Veni Creator*. While she was free to fly around the cloister garth, the gentle bird always returned to her master's humble cell. One day, after the kitchen supply of corn had run out, and the brother cook had scoured the big empty urn that served for a bin, Father Trujillo came begging for a bit of ground corn for his "little daughter," as he called the dove. When the cook said that there was no grain left, Fray José told him to look again, and, of course, the urn was filled to the

From Toledo

top. This tale resembled the old water miracles of Calonga and of the ship at sea, but, because of the dove's connection, had more of the savor of the *Little Flowers* of his Father St. Francis. And so it gained a greater circulation throughout the city and the great valley.

It so happened that an old friar from the custody of New Mexico came to San Cosme sometime thereafter. This man had known the martyred Fathers Letrado, Arvide, Miranda, and Porras, and was able to describe their work and their final sacrifice from firsthand knowledge of the land and its people. The result was that Father Trujillo's talk with Sor Juana de San Antonio, who most likely had already died within the past twenty years, swept back on his soul like a hurricane. But even if he did request to be sent to New Mexico, he was afraid that his age would be very much against him. Nonetheless, he casually broached the matter to his father provincial sometime later, while visiting the brethren at El Convento Grande, and the provincial, without the faintest sign of quibbling, kindly told him that he could go. The old man's first thought was to repair to the choir of San Francisco where, dropping to his knees, he made a deep-felt apology to old Mother Juana.

That same year he joined an armed party that happened to be going to New Mexico. Once more he embarked on another long voyage across another vast ocean, but this time it was a sea of long desert doldrums of sand and lofty waving mountains of stone.

* *   * *   * *   * *   * *   * *   * *

Old Fray José de Trujillo had been writing a letter the day two Zuñi runners came in with a written message from their own padre. Life was so serenely empty on the isolated cliff pueblos of Moqui, time so superabundant, that he had resumed an old habit of penning long letters to certain of his brethren at San Cosme and El Convento Grande. The letters were mostly spiritual in content, outpourings of his lonely meditations, since there was very little of the external world to report. Nothing ever happend on Xongopavi, or her four sister pueblos on their own rocky promontories. There were no excitable Europeans around to make news, or else manufacture some by way of gossip. His closest communicative neighbor, the friar of Zuñi, was several days away—except for fleet Indian runners. While the villa of Santa Fe and the homesteads of Spaniards along the Rio del Norte lay almost a hundred leagues across a danger-fraught wilderness.

A chattering commotion among the children of Xongopavi made Father Trujillo lay down his turkey quill and come out stooping from his little cell of stone and mud. Some naked boys were pointing out the barely discernible figures of two strangers on the desert floor far below, approaching the mesa from the direction of Zuñi. For a moment, he got the feeling of standing on the high stern of a great anchored galleon and watching an outrigger gliding in from a far island shore. Then he smiled to himself, wondering how he could explain to these simple children of the desert how their primitive counterparts of the South Sea islands lived. He kept on relishing this thought during the good while it took the newcomers, a pair of Zuñi youths, to climb the cliff and explain their business to the watchful "old men" of the village. Then they came up to him and delivered a small folded piece of paper which the father of Zuñi had sent.

For a long time Father Trujillo stood motionless on the flat sunny rock after reading the message over and over. Then he hied

From Toledo

himself back into his cell and picked up his quill again. His gaunt hand began scribbling excitedly, this time putting down a piece of most extraordinary news which had originated in the capital of the kingdom—good tidings indeed to his fervent soul. The core of it was that *"a girl of ten (the high sheriff's daughter, who was crippled with the gravest pains) had commended herself to an image of* Nuestra Señora del Sagrario de Toledo *which she had before her, and suddenly she found herself cured. And, filled with wonder over the miracle, she said that the Virgin had told her: 'Child, arise and say that this Custody will soon find itself destroyed, because of the little reverence it has for my priests, and that this miracle will be testimony to this truth; that they must amend their fault if they do not wish to undergo the punishment.' The event was publicized, and a Mass with a sermon was sung, the child being present. They burned complaints and lawsuits which lay in the archive against the priests."*

Father Trujillo knelt in prayer for a long time afterward, occasionally offering an apology to Sor Juana de San Antonio. Then he went out on the cliff's rocky deck to watch the diminishing figures of the Zuñi runners already a league away. Could it be that this vast peaceful world of Moqui, so still that one's ears sometimes seemed to catch the rumble of the ocean sea on the other side of the globe—could it be that it did nurture an explosive force within its cold stone heart? He thought of Father Porras, the wonderworking first missionary to these very pueblos, who had been poisoned by the jealous *caciques* forty years ago. But even his death for Christ was of a quiet nature, not the loud and bloody thing one associated with martyrdom, like those colorful executions in ancient Rome or in the kingdom of Japan.

The people themselves were as inscrutable as the land in their slow silent ways. Diminutive and very poor, they even called themselves the *hopi,* or the peaceful ones. These included the dwellers of the four other cliff promontories on which their pueblos were perched, for the custody at this time did not have enough friars to staff the missions established on each of them. And peaceful was the right term for all these aborigines, who seemed to exist in a kind of tepid somnolence, neither hot enough to become fervent Christians, nor steely cold enough to rise up and kill for their pagan beliefs, like the old Romans or the Nipponese. The only times he had seen them come to life was for their stolid monotonous dances, especially one type which they once let him see on the rock of Gualpi, when the medicinemen and their disciples came out prancing, hideously daubed with colored clays all over their naked bodies, and carrying enormous writhing snakes clamped in their underslung jaws. The spectacle had made him weep with sadness, for it vividly showed him the firm hold which the infernal serpent had on these benighted people.

That he would never make true Christians out of the *hopi,* in the few years left to him, Father Trujillo had been sure. And that they would turn on him and slay him for being a servant of the true God, this had seemed just as unlikely; for they were actually fond of him in their own undemonstrative way, perhaps because they did not consider him too much of a threat to their pagan customs. His abandonment of all hope of martyrdom had not been born of bitterness or frustration, however. Cynicism was a stranger to his character. On the contrary, he was completely resigned to the fate of dying a peaceful and uneventful death.

What had sealed this resigned conviction was his posthumous encounter with Fray Bernardo de Marta, soon after he came to the custody. While he was being escorted to his first mission of San

From Toledo

Diego de Jémez, the party paused to rest at the pueblo of Zia along the way. The friar of this mission showed him the grave of Fray Bernardo, dead for more than thirty years already, but still much alive in the memories of all the colonists, and the Zia Indians, as a genuine saint. His story was utterly simple, but beautiful with meaning. Bernardo and his brother Juan had entered the Franciscan Order in the convent of Zamora in Galicia, in 1597—the very year the Blessed Felipe de Jesús was crucified in Japan. After they were ordained together, the two Marta brothers asked to be sent together to the Far East, inspired, as young Trujillo was, by the first martyrs of Japan. Upon their arrival in the City of Mexico in 1605, Fray Juan de Marta was allowed to continue on his way to the Philippines and Japan, but his brother Fray Bernardo was ordered to stay behind in New Spain. He was subsequently assigned to the friary at Puebla de los Angeles—where Trujillo himself asked for the garb of St. Francis almost thirty years later.

It was the first time in their lives that these two brothers had ever been separated. And for Fray Bernardo there was the further disappointment of losing all hope of attaining martyrdom in the company of his beloved brother. Sometime later, Bernardo was dispatched to the custody of New Mexico, where he received the pueblo of Zia as his mission. Meanwhile, his lucky brother Juan, after laboring for a relatively short time in Japan, was beheaded at Meaco on August the sixteenth, 1618. Father Bernardo de Marta, however, spent a quarter of a century all alone in Zia, endearing himself to his people while he endured all manner of hardships with a cheerful spirit, until his edifying death on September the eighteenth, 1635.

A question which came up in Father Trujillo's mind while

kneeling by the lonely grave at Zia was this: "Which of the two Marta brothers was the greater martyr and saint—Fray Juan who was beheaded very early in his missionary career, or Fray Bernardo who had gladly obeyed like a staunch soldier of God, and then had endured the daily martyrdoms of a long and stern life of duty through the dry and desolate years? This thought had followed Fray José de Trujillo from that day on, through his stay at Jémez to his final assignment to this province of Moqui two years ago. A custodial chapter held at Jémez itself in August, 1672, had selected him to evangelize a pagan tribe living in the extreme western wilderness on the way to the South Sea. For a brief time the prophecy of Mother Juana had flared up anew, only to die out completely when, due to a serious shrinking of personnel in the custody, he was sent to peaceful Xongopavi instead. But he was content.

Only now, as he lingered gazing far out upon the desert, after the Zuñi messengers were out of sight, and as the thin wavy line of blue mountains in the far horizon began looking more and more like islands at the other edge of a yellow sea, did he apologize to Sor Juana de San Antonio once more with a new upsurge of expectancy. At this moment her old abandoned prophecy seemed to fuse with the very recent prediction of Our Lady of Toledo in one burning glare, like the throbbing sun which beat down upon his baldish head and the hot rock ledge under his sandals, and made the desert sands far below shine golden like the peaceful South Sea at sunset.

There came to him also, out of that same glare, a most un-fortunate incident which he had banished from his mind the day

he heard it. Only a few years ago, here in Moqui, a most im-
prudent and, particularly in his case, an unworthy son of the
gentle St. Francis—very likely an ex-soldier whose novitiate and
clerical training at El Convento Grande had failed to erase a
certain brutal streak—had caused a backsliding *hopi* neophyte to
be flogged so severely that he died as a result of it. Indeed, whether from good or from evil, the precedents for possible martyrdom
were here.

And now this unmistakeable token through the high sheriff's
daughter to all the friars and the colonists of the kingdom. The
Spanish people had taken the warning seriously to heart and had
begun mending their ways, it was true, and thus they might avert
their own destruction because of their contrition. But the an-
nihilation of the custody and kingdom was definitely assured, if
he had gotten the rumor correctly.

2.   BLACK GOD OF PO-HE-YEMU

During the summer of 1680 the twin-pueblo of Taos was a
picture of that abiding peaceableness with which its gently arch-
ing mountain naturally endowed the two great mud tenements
nestling at its cool green base. A pleasant crystal stream purling
down from a rich jade fold in the blue-green sweep of rising peak
separated these two tenements, or apartments. The north one,
especially, its dun terraces rising five storeys high in an uneven
pyramid, repeated the staid aloofness of the towering mountain
behind it; the recessed tiers of ochre walls provided their own
restful complement to the imperceptibly changing blues and greens

soaring beyond. Occasional white-sheeted figures, standing or squatting motionless on one or the other terrace, or seen crossing with the slow pace of dream from one tenement to the other, furthered this spell of quietude, at once comfortable and secure.

To the Spanish *alcalde* or overseer, in his own single-storeyed adobe home not far away, there was no real reason for suspecting anything untoward among the Indians of Taos. There was no sullen show of resentment, for example, as had been reported of late from certain southern pueblos, like Jémez and San Juan. The three other Spanish families living next door, who with the *alcalde* kept large herds and flocks of livestock all over the grassy valley, felt a fraternal closeness with the pueblo's people, since both formed a needed bastion against the savage Utes to the north. This nomadic tribe was in the habit of staging a raid about once a year for booty in maize or horses if not for the sheer love of fighting and collecting a few scalps. Nearby in the fortress-visaged mission of San Gerónimo with its single solid square tower, the two friars—a priest and his laybrother companion—also looked upon the scene with a quiet satisfaction, for the Indians were attending Mass and the catechism reasonably well. This common Christian bond contributed to the prevailing sence of security.

It was true that during this particular summer an unusual number of Indian leaders from diverse pueblos had been seen frequenting their faraway northern Tigua sister. Their red blankets and bulky nape-hairknots made them most noticeable among the taller thin-braided Taos men in white. Very often seen about was that Popé of San Juan, whom the Spaniards knew for a trouble maker; he was considered more or less harmless and without much influence, but still a gadfly to the authorities. But everyone knew that in certain years, for reasons known only to the Indian mind, there were extra meetings held in different pueblos by the "old men." It had to do with matters of rain, people said. At any rate, Indians were crazy about such *juntas*. Since nothing really detrimental to Spanish rule came out of them, they had long been countenanced as a matter of course, like the open decent dances which the friars did not class among the forbidden *cachinas*.

It was also common knowledge that a great spirit reputedly dwelt inside a hidden *estufa* of Taos. He was the *teniente* or executive of a much greater spirit, the great and good Po-he-yemu, who was the guardian of the ancient ways of the pueblos. But the *teniente* himself was of a more fearsome mien and disposition; he was said to be gigantic in size and very black all over, and his big and bulging yellow eyes were said to penetrate a person's very breast. Indian mothers in all the pueblos scared their children when they were naughty with the mere mention of him, while Spanish women all over the kingdom had also become accustomed to threatening their unruly offspring with this bogeyman.

For such he was to adult Spaniards, generally—one of many Indian myths and no more. The colonists more readily believed that each pueblo kept an enormous rattlesnake hidden within some *estufa*, and that it thrived on the sacrifices of tender babies; otherwise, how else explain the fact that these Indians, while having infants as frequently as the Spaniards, still did not increase in population? But the right-hand man of Po-he-yemu was only a word in the maw of superstition, just a false and non-existent god, or at most a manifestation of the devil himself, as Spaniards looked upon such things.

Yet, in reality, there was no peace at all deep inside the north tenement of Taos. A volcano was actually throbbing there, even if not visible or audible to the ordinary folk of the village. To them the casual visits of Popé and other medicinemen from many other pueblos, even if more frequent than usual, were ordinary pilgrimages such as many Indians made to hidden little shrines among the hills and *arroyos*, except that these leaders sought the supreme shrine of Po-he-yemu. Nor did these privileged *caciques* and their *principales*—who headed the many secret intermingling societies of pueblo theocracy—see any physical stirring along the dark labyrinths leading into the bowels of the tenement. The big round chamber itself was as silent as a cave within a mountain's bosom. They saw only the immense bulk of a man, buried in the folds of his great blanket, as he sat haunched and cross-legged before a very small fire in the middle of the hard earthen floor.

The tiny flame made the *teniente* seem bigger, by casting his shadow in giant wraiths upon the whitewashed arc of wall behind him, and across the thick *vigas* directly over his large white-haired skull. The coarse strands on his wide scalp were parted in the middle, in the Ute-borrowed fashion of the north Tiguas of Taos and Picuris, and fell over either shoulder in two tightly braided quirts, like stiff snakes. His low cavernous voice, rumbling up softly from deep inside his ample blanket, spoke forth in brief calm sentences—now in Tigua, now in Tehua, or in Tano, or in Quéres—as he turned his large yellow eyes for the moment (and they did shine in the firelight like a puma's or a bobcat's) on the individual visiting chief he was addressing.

The real turmoil was inside that big head, reaching far down into that huge chest under the blanket, but not even the large countenance betrayed a trace of it. To the awed guests before him it was a stolid Indian face, already seamed deeply across the net of lesser wrinkles by immemorial moons, barely suggesting that the skin had once been very black in tone as well as smooth,

From Toledo

much darker and shinier than that of the pueblo people. The un-remembered years of squatting in gloomy darkness had also helped to bleach it well. What this oracle of the great Po-he-yemu said to his visitors did bear a promise of violence, of fearsome destruction for the Spaniards and their oppressive religion. But Popé and his fellow shamans of other pueblos, believing that the message emanat-ed through him from the silent netherworld of Xipapu—whence all Indians came and where they returned after death—had no way of knowing or suspecting that it boiled out of an inner furnace of a personal hate stronger than death.

For Diego de Santiago, or Naranjo, had never forgotten his own identity, or the bitter circumstances that had made him what he was, although by now he felt himself every inch an Indian of the pueblos. More than that, he reveled with a delirious secret satisfac-tion in his long-held position as custodian of pueblo lore and rites, as the supreme coaxer of the unseen powers, even if he had to wield this influence under the anonymity of mystery. The colorful highlights of his entire life had kept simmering in his mind during the dark days and the dark nights all through the recurring seasons of many years, feeding his hate while he fed the sacred fire be-fore him or the little fetishes at his side.

The very, very old *principales* of Taos, who knew that he was a black man from New Spain with the Spanish name of Diego Naranjo when he first came to the pueblo, were dead for many years now. The awe-filled medicinemen of later generations knew him only as a shaman and sorcerer far superior to any of their very best, one who really "knew." The Taos headmen of the secret societies could only say that he had dwelt among them from days unremembered, silently tending the sacred fire and "feeding" the holy scalps and "the little people" in a basket beside him, for which the natives provided the meat from the communal rabbit hunts. They saw him when he issued instructions, or when he recounted for hours on end the age-long myths of the pueblos which he had come to embellish from other legends that he knew, or from his own rich fancy. And only these "old men" had ever seen him face to face. For Diego only stirred outside at night or, if during early daylight hours or at dusk, hiding his features well within the hood made by his blanket. A few of the ordinary people of Taos swore that they had once seen his yellow eyes just for a fleeting moment.

It all made him feel divine, as a matter of fact, infinitely greater than any witchdoctor he had watched perform with so much awe when he was a boy in Veracruz. This divine vesture was worth all the pains and humiliations which a man of his own race could ever suffer at the hands of arrogant white masters. Only the crown of just retribution was wanting, and this source of complete satisfaction, after these many long years of patient waiting, now lay within his power to inflict.

Diego had been born on the east coast of New Spain of a Negro mother whom he barely remembered. The only clear picture left of her was that of a thin black woman sobbing most fearfully and dolorously under a clump of wide banana fronds, her bare shoulders and back glistening red from a cruel lashing. Nor had Diego ever known for sure if his father was a Spaniard, an Aztec, or a Tlascalan. Most likely the man was a *mestizo*. In his first years Diego's hair had straightened out and grown long, somewhat like an Indian's; but his darkening skin tended more toward charcoal than to the tone of reddish brown earth, and his big round eyes

From Toledo

were yellowish instead of brown or black, so that not only the Spaniards, but his own fellow slaves and other dark acquaintances said that he was a *mulato*. He also grew very fast, around the time a new master took him to the valley of Mexico. At fifteen he was bigger and more muscular than the average Spaniard or Indian of the great valley.

Ever since he was a small boy the fathers had taught him the catechism, and they marveled at the way he could repeat the longest prayers and the hardest answers after hearing them only once.

It was the same in learning how to write. Diego had liked these kind priests for the interest they showed in his talents. But as he grew older, his mind could not take those senseless Christian commandments which forbade so many fine pleasures under the pain of eternal hellfire and, what was worse, under penalty of a whipping in this present life. And such whippings were not for white transgressors, but for the dark people only.

Diego much rather enjoyed learning other teachings and practices, in the talk of old black men, both slaves and free men, which brought up in his head the most fascinating pictures about a faraway land which was called Africa. It was his own mother's homeland, he was told. It was from the coasts of Guinea that she and thousands of other black people had been brought herded in great ships, not so much like cattle, but like pigs in pokes. Many died on the way. Diego's storytellers took him at night to very secret gatherings in the forests, to hear more jungle lore and to watch the witchdoctors perform. They were a wondrous sight to see in their hideous masks and tropical plumes. Their magic astounded him as it did the others—but only the first few times, for his fast eye caught the cleverest tricks, and his quick hands could repeat them perfectly when he tried them alone.

He also found friends among the lowliest of the Indians in the *barrios* of the City of Mexico. Certain ones among the Aztecs also held on to the secret ways of their ancients, and they took Diego to their secret meetings. But their magic was poor, certainly nothing to compare with what he had learned from the witchdoctors of his own people. These Indians' stories, however, were most interesting. The one which impressed him the most concerned their great Father Huitzilopochtli. He had come from a mysterious paradise far to the north of New Spain, and had founded the great city of the Aztecs on a beautiful lake where he saw an eagle clutching a serpent with its claws and beak. These Indians insisted that there also was a great and beautiful lake, called Copala, in that far northern region; they also said that Aztec people still dwelt there undisturbed, as in the old days before the Spaniards came.

This impressed Diego the most because such a fabulous land, unlike the Africa of his mother and people, might well be reached by foot, there being no ocean to cross. It was uppermost in his mind the day he attached himself to a supply train departing for the kingdom of New Mexico. The *mestizo* and *mulato* drivers of the ox-teams hid him in a cart until the caravan was a week away from the valley. Then one of the mulattoes passed him off as his son, and the escorting soldiers, who were from New Mexico, never suspected that he was a fugitive slave. Once in that New Mexico, Diego would look for the region of Copala where no master would ever find him, and where he would never again hear the padres forbidding the best things of life as a sin and a crime.

He was greatly disappointed with the villa of Santa Fe. Here was the same life of New Spain, though in a much meaner scale and style, the Spaniards still lording it over the dark folk. Here were the same priests making one attend the daily *doctrina*, to hear about sin and punishment. The Mexican Indians of Analco only laughed when he inquired discreetly about the Lake of Copala. If there was such a place, they said, not even the venturesome Spaniards had found it. Realizing that he had placed his trust in a mere fable, Diego resolved to remain in this isolated kingdom, but he began looking for a way to avoid living in Analco; it savored too much of the old *barrios* that he knew back in New Spain. Besides, someone coming up from the City of Mexico might recognize him for a runaway servant if he stayed in the villa. At this point his brawn and intelligent ways had caught the eye of the *maese de campo*, Don Pedro de Chávez. As he could see that the smiling field commander of the militia readily took him for a fugitive, Diego promptly offered him his free services. And as he had expected, Don Pedro dispatched him forthwith to his cattle hacienda many leagues south of the villa. The homestead was called El Tunque, from the wide and sandy *arroyo* of this name which joined the Rio del Norte near the Indian pueblo of San Felipe. These Indians of San Felipe were the only neighbors.

Diego Naranjo came to like his new *patrón* very much. For Don Pedro was a fine *señor*, who placed him soon after in charge of the herdsmen of his many cattle, horses, and sheep. Diego also liked him for his person—the only Spaniard he ever did really like in his entire life. Don Pedro had the air and stoop of a gentleman, whom all the colonists addressed as "Don," like the lord governor himself, yet he was easygoing with his servants. He did not abuse them or other people of humble caste as did the petty officials he had known in New Spain. Diego was also most gratified to discover that his new *patrón* could not be manhandled by the mission friars, nor intimidated by them like most other captains of the kingdom.

It was in the year 1621, shortly after his arrival, Diego clearly

remembered, that there was a long and furious fight between Governor Eulate and the missionaries. By this time, Diego was in complete charge of the Tunque hacienda for his master, since Don
Pedro was occupied in the capital with the troops, or else out on
a campaign. Diego had a little house of his own, and also a hard-
working wife; for the *maese* had graciously allowed him to marry
a woman from the pueblo of San Felipe nearby. Through her,
Diego had also begun to learn the Quéres language of San Felipe
very fast, and he was even admitted into the councils of the
cacique at San Felipe, for he had shown him an extra voodoo
trick or two which his own *na'hua-i* or witchdoctors did not
know. At this time the south Tiguas of Sandia and the Quéres
of San Felipe had been missing Mass and the catechism because of
the many *cachina* dances being held that year. When the friars
complained to the lord governor, Eulate sent Don Pedro de Chávez to look into the matter, since Don Pedro was also in complete
charge of those two pueblos. The friars demanded that he destroy
the *estufas* forthwith and have the pagan leaders flogged. But Don
Pedro merely chided the Indians for missing Mass and let it go
at that. Right away Father Zambrano and others began writing
letters to New Spain, and telling all over the custody, that the
maese de campo himself was counseling the Indians to disobey the
fathers. But it did not seem to bother Don Pedro.

This incomparable master died four or five years later, unfortunately. Don Fernando de Chávez, his eldest son and heir, was
altogether different. He always sided with the friars whenever
there was a dispute of this kind between them and other lord
governors who came later. Not holding the high position of field
commander like his father, Don Fernando lived with his family
at El Tunque, from where he kept a close eye on the pueblos

From Toledo

of San Felipe and Sandia. This is why Diego finally left the hacienda and went to live secretly in the pueblo of Alameda further
south, after Don Fernando punished him for having danced in
a *cachina*. Diego's own wife was chiefly to blame, for she had
listened so much to the Christian dribble of Don Fernando's mother
and wife that she reported him to his master.

Another Spaniard whom Diego Naranjo had fiercely come to
hate was Captain Bartolomé Romero, the first of this name. He
had also hated this man's son and grandson for the same reasons,
all of whom were now dead. While Diego was living in Alameda,
the Indians of that pueblo held a *cachina* inside their mission
church one night, as its missionary lived in Sandia. After the main
dancing was over, and everybody had laid the sacred masks away,
and the *hot'canyi* in the high pulpit was screaming himself into
a faint in order to talk with the other-world spirits—and Diego
was waiting eagerly for the head *quirena's* signal for each man to
grab the woman nearest him—that hateful Captain Romero burst in
with a squad of soldiers. They drove the people out of the church,
beating them with their whips and with the flat of their swords. It
was here that Diego decided to disassociate himself from the hated
Spaniards forever.

It was here, too, and in Sandia, that Diego had learned to
speak the Tigua tongue, just as easily as he had learned Spanish
and Aztec as a lad, and then Quéres at San Felipe. He had
picked up some Tehua also, from a man from Santa Clara living
at San Felipe. For he could learn languages as quickly as he had
learned sleight-of-hand from watching the witchdoctors in Veracruz. The Tigua tongue proved the most useful, for shortly after
that, Diego disappeared from Alameda also, and made his way
secretly to Taos. This mountain pueblo was not only far away from

the villa of Santa Fe as well as the rest of the Indian villages, and very difficult to reach in the long winter months, but the Tigua people there had more spirit than the Tehuas or the Quéres, or their fellow Tiguas in the warmer lower valleys.

Nor did he have any qualms about abandoning his San Felipe wife at El Tunque, and their two little boys, Pascual and Bartolomé. (Don Pedro's wife gave them these names because they were born on the feasts of these saints, and Diego had always despised the younger boy's name, for a good reason.) His Indian wife had become too much of a Christian and had been getting steadily worse, like others among her people. As for the boys, they were Diego's by siring only. At the time they had no place in his heart, perhaps because he himself, besides lacking a father, had been obliged to fend for himself since childhood. It was also the way of the brave animals of the forest, he had long ago observed. But with the years his human heart had begun to tend toward his sons, making him inquire as to their present lot. And sometimes his human reason let them share vaguely in his future dreams.

Although Diego had not seen his family since the day he left it, he had gathered a few facts in recent years, by the same secret and devious means by which he informed himself of the state of the whole kingdom. He knew that his San Felipe wife, now old and sickly, still lived in the humble dwelling he himself had built by the old Tunque hacienda; the house stood by itself now, since the son of the late Don Fernando had abandoned the place and moved the Chávez homestead further south to Bernalillo. His wife had married again, this time an Indian of her own tribe, since both the Spaniards and the Indians thought that he, Diego Naranjo, had run away after the Romero affair at Alameda, and had perished like all other fugitives in the perilous *Jornada del Muerto* on the way

From Toledo

to New Spain. (Popé had informed Diego that ten years ago a German travelling merchant had perished on this desert stretch between Socorro and Guadalupe del Paso. This foreigner was said to have practiced magic among the colonists and the friars had him imprisoned; but he ran away, and his sun-dried corpse was found weeks later in that deadly area. Since then it had been called "The Dead Man's Route." Diego would have liked to meet the man, since he might have learned some new tricks.)

His wife's San Felipe husband had died, leaving her with two young Indian sons. The two older boys by Diego were now grown men. Pascual Naranjo was the herdsman for a prosperous colonist of the Rio Abajo, and married to a servant woman called "La Cota." Bartolomé Naranjo, who took care of his aged mother and his two young half-brothers, spent long periods working for the families of the Spanish officials in Santa Fe.

Diego also had a young son in Taos, and a number of older daughters, by the Tigua widow of Taos who used to cook his meals. She was now dead. The woman had taken her successive babies to be baptized by the padre of San Gerónimo, as all infants of the pueblo were. Diego had not kept track of the girls, now grown women themselves and perhaps married, but he knew that the son's name was "José," and could recognize him among the youths of Taos. José looked very Castilian, which made his mates nickname him "*Castera*," and this made Diego suspect that his own father might have been a Spaniard of Veracruz. The friar of Taos had always liked the boy José, and had taught him to read and to speak Spanish well, but still Diego was sure that the priest had always pitied the lad a little for being what the Spaniards and their prim religion called a bastard. This was all very well, for the time being, but the day would come when young José Naranjo of Taos, and also his older half-brothers Pascual and Bartolomé Naranjo of the Rio Abajo, would be proud to learn that the *teniente* of Po-he-yemu—the genius who had succeeded in annihilating the Spanish kingdom and custody—was their very own father. Then *they* would be lords and princes, no less. But for the present he had no time to dally with offspring.

On first coming to Taos, Diego Naranjo had gone directly to the heads of the curing societies, or rather it was these *principales* who had apprehended him right away to inquire about his stealthy arrival. Right away he astounded them with feats of legerdemain which made their own appear crude and childish. They took him immediately for a superior sort of being, as he had expected. They also marveled greatly at his command of the language of the Spaniards and the Quéres as well as their own Tigua tongue. When he told them that he also knew the Aztec language of Po-he-yemu, which he did, they were sure that a powerful nether-world spirit or *xihuana* dwelt in him. For only the spirits knew all tongues. Without any formal ceremony, Diego was initiated into all the secret societies. And when the old *cacique* died a year or two afterward, they could consider no one but himself to take his place. Ordinarily the war captains could admonish or even castigate the *cacique* if he did not fast or pray right for his people, but what war captain dared even question a *cacique* who was, at the same time, the *teniente* or lieutenant of the great Po-he-yemu himself?

The doctrine and character of Po-he-yemu had been a welcome windfall for Diego, although not altogether unexpected. He had already discovered that the pueblos of this region regarded Moc-

From Toledo

tezuma or some such god of the Aztecs as a powerful and bene-volent spirit, although they could not pronounce his name correctly. With them it was *Po-he-yemu, Po-se-yemu, Po-se-ueve,* or *Pa-ya-temu,* according to the various tribes. Mexican Indians brought by the Spaniards since early times must have told them about the kingly founder of the Aztec nation, how he had been born in this north country. By now these pueblos held it as an ancient teaching of theirs that he was their own spirit father dwelling in Xipapu, a place in the bowels of the earth whence they had sprung. Evidently they had confounded this Xipapu with Copala. The Tiguas of Taos, he soon learned, identified it with their sacred azure lake on top of their beautiful mountain. And because Diego knew the Aztec story in better detail, and after noticing his hosts' astonishment at his knowledge of the god's own tongue, not to mention Diego's great size and his astounding magic, he had them concluding that he also spoke with the god on occasion—in fact, was his lieutenant come back to the upper earth in order to guide the destinies of the pueblo people and to restore the purity of their ancient ways. However, it was a secret for the exclusive eyes and ears of those who "knew," the headman of each pueblo.

Thus, for almost forty years now, the north *estufa* of Taos had been an oracle for the religious pagan leaders of the pueblos. The secret of Diego's existence therein had eventually filtered down among the ordinary pueblo folk, and even among the Spanish colonists, but in such legendary form that it helped rather than hindered the power of his position. The present description of himself was that of decades ago when his skin was smooth and firm, while anyone outside who once knew Diego Naranjo, the big mulatto, had either died or had long ago given him up for a dead fugitive. The other pueblo chiefs who came to consult with him in the *estufa,* including Popé, took him for a full-blooded Indian of Taos, albeit possessing the most extraordinary supernatural powers and knowledge.

What Popé and the others were now consulting him about, and with the utmost secrecy, was something he had patiently nur- tured through the years: the total destruction of the Spaniards in the region, and most especially the missionaries and the churches. He had always been certain that the pueblo warriors,· if they should unite and fight as one, could easily destroy the relatively small Spanish colony, in spite of its superiority in horses and fire-arms. But he had found it next to impossible to unite the pueblos' forces, divided as these many villages were—not only by language, but by certain minor feuds of age-long standing. Moreover, the pueblo men as a whole were no real fighters, nor even superior hunters, like the Apaches and Utes and other nomadic Indians of the wide spaces who lived from the chase and from raids on their more peaceful neighbors. The peacefulness of the stunted pueblos had long been bred into them through a blunting sedentary life of corn- planting and year-round ceremonials. They also lived in peace with each other as individuals because of a strong underlying feeling that one's neighbor might be a powerful witch in disguise, and therefore most dangerous to cross. To perform some act of violence, the pueblo men had to work themselves into a fighting pitch by dancing and other rituals. The warlike tribes did this also, but they required less of the medicine.

Some years after Diego took up his lodging in Taos, the Indians of Jémez (who had more spirit for being mountain people) de- cided to rebel against the Spaniards. Even then they had to enlist the aid of the Navajo Apaches, whose sole interest lay in capturing horses. They succeeded in killing one lone Spanish soldier—Diego remembered this because the victim's surname happened to be Naranjo like his own. Promptly, Governor Arguello went over to Jémez and hanged twenty-nine of their leaders. He also had forty others of that pueblo fearfully lashed and placed in fetters. This incident taught Diego from the very beginning that he had to proceed with the most extreme caution, if his own plan was to succeed some day. It also taught him to remain anonymously legendary in the background, to escape punishment or even death if his efforts were thwarted. Besides, this secrecy made him feel all the more divine.

His own first major attempt took place about ten years later, in 1650, in the days of Governor Concha. After holding many long councils with the *caciques* and *principales* of all the pueblos, and one roving Apache chieftain, he sent out two painted deer-skins from Taos, each to be passed through the western and eastern groups of pueblos, and telling the exact day in which each village was to pounce on its mission friar and on any other Spaniards in the vicinity. The warriors of the pueblos closest to Santa Fe would then surround the capital and squeeze its entire population to death. The date set was Holy Thursday, when most Spaniards, and the friar in each mission, would be holding vigil in church. But for some unaccountable reason, several pueblos refused to act at the very last moment, even the Moqui pueblos who had been the most dissatisfied with the missionaries. As a result, the few pueblos which did rise in rebellion soon felt the heavy hand of Governor Concha, who hanged many leaders at Isleta, Alameda, Cochiti, San Felipe, and Jémez.

But no one suspected where, or by whom, the plot had been hatched.

When some leaders of the punished pueblos came to remonstrate with Diego, he showed them plainly that it was not Po-he-yemu himself who had failed them, but that it was the fault of those several pueblos which had shown themselves to have the heart of a rabbit. Nevertheless, he could not get them to plot again after that. It took many years for these frightful memories of Governor Concha to die out. Diego did succeed at different times in having this or that individual friar or soldier killed, his message from Po-he-yemu always going forth through many scat-tered messengers so that the incident could not be traced back to himself. If the culprit was caught and then confessed that the spirits had ordered him to slay, the Spaniards had no way of pursuing what they considered a myth. But this could not be at-tempted too often; the danger of discovery was too great for the small damage done to the Spaniards.

Once again, in 1664, Diego made another major attempt, but employing different tactics. Although he well knew that the Piro tribe far to the southeast in the plains of the Salinas or salt pools, and their relations at Socorro and Senecú by the Rio del Norte, were much devoted to their fathers, having never rebuilt their *estufas*, he planted a revolt among them when a few hardy Piro medicinemen came to consult with Po-he-yemu. If they killed four or five missionaries, and a dozen or so Spaniards there, it was worth the effort. An uprising at the southernmost extremity of the kingdom should not be so easily traced to Taos. Again, Diego counseled getting aid from the Apaches with promises of free horses, and to attack on the night of Holy Thursday. The plot went awry, however, and the Piro leaders were hanged.

As the older *principales* died off in the pueblos, the newer ones kept coming up to Taos in increasing numbers, but only to learn at firsthand the mystifying tricks of their trade. Diego would

From Toledo

sound them out occasionally on Po-he-yemu's prime wish, but they did not want to hear of this. The Spanish guns and swords were much too powerful against stones and arrows and *macanas;* their bullwhips especially were too terrible to contemplate. All they wanted to know was how to draw lizards and little balls of hair, and bits of wool or flint, from the breasts and bellies of sick people in a thoroughly convincing manner. They wanted to know how to make people think that they actually saw little *cachina* dolls scurrying through the pueblo alleys at night. And most of all, they wanted to "know" the astounding medicine by which one be-witched an enemy into sickness. One made very little dolls, in which some hair or nail parings of a particular person were imbedded; then one stuck the doll with a cactus thorn, with appropriate chants, on the head or on the stomach, and that certain person fell gravely ill with the severest head or belly aches.

Not long after he taught this medicine to some sorcerers of the Tehua valley, it caused a most welcome disturbance which he had not foreseen. There was a noisy friar at San Ildefonso by the name of Fray Andrés Durán. He started complaining that he and his brother and his brother's wife had been bewitched by the Indian medicinemen. The affliction spread in such proportions among other Spaniards and Christian Indians, that forty-seven leaders from San Juan and the four other Tehua pueblos were arrested by that new Captain Xavier and hauled off in shackles to Santa Fe. Four of these were hanged, and the rest were kept imprisoned in the capital by Governor Treviño.

Angered and alarmed by such a thorough round-up of their societies' headmen, the warriors of the Tehuas got together, danced themselves into a frenzy of bravery one night, and on the following day appeared at the palace of the lord governor. They had all kinds of products to barter for the release of the prisoners; but they also were in war-paint, carrying their weapons and leather shields. Governor Treviño refused what he considered a bribe, but released the prisoners; yet he was also curious to know why so many warriors had come as though ready for combat. The fearless reply was that they had come prepared to kill his lordship and as many Spaniards as they could before they themselves were killed.

Among these prisoners was Popé. The incident showed Diego that the pueblos were not cowards, that they could muster enough spirit and unity if properly aroused. It also brought Popé to his attention as a good prospect for helping him carry out his master plan.

This had happened only five years ago. And only a year before that, a rumor had come out of the villa of Santa Fe, to the effect that the Virgin Mother Mary had foretold the complete destruction of the Spaniards. Diego had put much stock in the reputed prophecy, for in his mind all mysterious things were true. It gave some tangible evidence that the powers behind the Christian religion were beginning to cede to those of the dark ancient people. But while the Spaniards regarded the wild Apaches as their real threat, not the ever disunited and habitually peaceful pueblos, Diego saw the threat already beginning to materialize among these mission Indians in their midst.

Since then the surprisingly brave anger displayed by the Tehuas before Governor Treviño had spread to all the other pueblos. It was because their *estufas*, as well as their secret little shrines by streams and mesas, were being destroyed right and left by orders of Don Antonio de Otermín, the new lord governor in Santa Fe. Those carrying out the orders with such fury were three hated

From Toledo

captains: Xavier, Quintana, and López Sambrano. The first two had come directly from Spain across the great sea, and they hated the very mention of Indian beliefs; the third was a native Spaniard of Santa Fe who welcomed any excuse for inflicting pain on others. These three furies were the most hated of all the Spaniards. It seemed most clear to Diego Naranjo, already approaching his eightieth year according to his own general reckoning, that his day for complete revenge was fast arriving at last. The medicine-men who came to see him showed the utmost interest in the wishes of Po-he-yemu, his own dear plan to exterminate the Spaniards and every vestige of their religion.

The most interested was Popé. Diego did not consider him enough of a leader to work out strategy or to persuade the pueblos to unite. He was not too popular among his own people of San Juan, what with his murder of its civil governor, who was also the husband of his own daughter, even though he had killed him because of his too close friendship with the Spaniards. But Popé showed spirit, and his hate approached Diego's the closest. He also could carry out instructions faithfully. Properly directed, he could be the instrument for carrying out the fateful designs of Po-he-yemu. And if the attempt failed, Popé would bear the blame.

From then on Popé began spending much time in the north tenement of Taos, learning tactics in detail and helping to instruct the envoys who kept coming to the lofty pueblo by the beautiful mountain. All the pueblos sent representatives, except the Piros of Senecú and Socorro, and their cousins of the Salinas who had abandoned their old pueblos and were now living with them, for they seemed to have sold out completely to the Spanish God and Spanish ways.

To keep the plot from leaking out, only the *caciques* and the headmen of the secret societies were to know of it until the supreme moment. The civil governors and their *fiscales* were not to be trusted at all; theirs was a Spanish system which had nothing to do with the old ways, and most of them were much too friendly with the fathers and the Spanish officials, as Popé's son-in-law had been. A goodly number of the ordinary people, too, like Diego's own wife at San Felipe long ago, had gone completely over to the Christian God, no longer caring for the old ways and refusing to take part in the *cachinas*. Only on the night before the concerted attack, after the headmen had ordered all the men to do war dances, would they reveal their purpose and then recruit them for a holy war. They would be promised all the Spanish plunder which they could lay hands on, moreover. If anyone remonstrated, he was to be taken aside and executed right then and there.

The northern pueblos would take care of all the Spaniards in the Rio Arriba missions and haciendas from Taos down to Tesuque, and the pueblos to the south and west those Spaniards living in the Rio Abajo. The Pecos and the Galisteo basin pueblos would do away with their friars and the colonists of their area and then, re-inforced by an Apache contingent, would converge on the villa of Santa Fe from the south in a distracting tactic. A concerted move from the north by Tiguas and Tehuas and Jémez would then finish the villa. But the first important step was to kill the local padre and any other Spaniard living nearby or on a visit.

Naranjo suggested, moreover, that they take the younger Spanish women alive; to him, the rape of the white man's women was as sweet a revenge as the massacre of the men. After the fall

From Toledo

of Santa Fe, when the Spaniards were wiped out completely, the leaders would see to it that all the people washed away their Christian baptism in the rivers; every cross, even the smallest which the friars made the Indians wear on their necks, had to be burned. And it was of utmost importance to defecate upon the altars before the churches were burned down. Afterward, every man would have as many wives as he pleased—although here Diego noticed a disturbed look in the faces before him. He never could understand why the pueblo people were, by ancient custom, monogamous.

The day fixed upon was the eleventh of August, as Diego and the Spaniards reckoned the days and months. Instead of painted deerskins this time, which might fall into alien hands and arouse suspicion, two harmless-looking cords with knots would be carried by runners to every pueblo, the one of deerskin thong to the pueblos on the morning side of the great river, the one of yucca twine to those on the sunset side. The knots would tell the exact day to the leaders who knew the code. Fleet runners, stationed at pre-determined points, would pass on the cord in relays, so that they arrived at exactly the right time at each and every pueblo.

* *   * *   * *   * *   * *   * *   * *

Due to some senseless bungling by a pair of carelessly chosen young runners of Tesuque, Diego Naranjo was forced to anticipate the uprising by a day. It turned out to be a better one—a Sunday as well as the popular feast of St. Lawrence, when the Spaniards tended to let down their guard. For the first time in many years, Diego's great mouth distended fully to the hindmost molars in the evilest of grins, as the reports of the successful massacre of mission padres and hacienda families started coming in on each others' heels. From Taos to Pecos, from San Juan to San Ildefonso and Tesuque, from Santo Domingo to Jémez, and even from the faraway uncertain Moqui pueblos, there came the mouth-sweetening news of slaughter. Twenty-one missionaries had fallen in one happy swoop on that single day. All the Spanish colonists near the northern pueblos, except those of La Cañada who had sought refuge in the villa, were likewise cut down, their homesteads despoiled of all their coveted effects and livestock. Although the extreme Rio Abajo colonists and their friars escaped by the skin of their teeth, from poor co-ordination between the Quéres of San Felipe and the Tiguas of Sandia, they were now fleeing like scared jackrabbits out of the kingdom, never to return. The only Spaniards left, the cream of the despised crop, were now huddled in terror within the villa of Santa Fe.

The fate of the lord governor and his hateful captains could now await another day, two days, a whole week of days. The villa was like an over-ripe peach, ready to be plucked, or even fall of its own dead weight to the ground. The warriors of Pecos and the Tanos and Quéres of the Galisteo basin already had the word to attack from the south; while the colonial militia engaged them in combat, the northern Tehuas and Tiguas would pour in from the north and pluck the fruit ready for the eating.

And he himself, Diego Naranjo—the representative of Po-he-yemu to these stupid people of the pueblos—would personally witness the last agony of the just as stupid Spaniard and his religion.

PART THREE:

KINGDOM'S END

KINGDOM'S END

1. THE CONFUSED CHIEFTAIN

Juan el Tano was very much surprised, and also a little scared, when a soldier pushed through the crowded courtyard and laid a hand on his shoulder, saying that the lord governor wished to see him right away inside the palace. The events of the past five days, ever since the interrogation of the two really scared Tesuque youths, who divulged the plan of the rebellion—then the gory slaughter of the friar of Tesuque, and now the common rumor in Santa Fe that Juan's own people of Galisteo and the other Tano pueblos had likewise killed Father Bernal and the friars of Pecos and San Marcos—all this had served to set his own nerves on edge as much as those of the Spanish inhabitants of the villa and of the Mexican Indians of Analco with whom he lived.

Ever since Sunday, all the people of the villa and of Analco had been heaped and huddled together within the great compound enclosed by the palace and the presidio, upon the lord governor's orders. They felt like the cattle and horses herded in with them.

The Lady

Together with the colonists from La Cañada to the north who had come in this very morning, and those from Los Cerrillos by the south turquoise hills who had arrived last night, there were over a thousand human beings packed inside the enclosure. Including the presidio soldiers, there were less than a hundred men and older boys found able to manage fire-arms, after weapons and ammunition had been broken out of the armory. Since then, parapets and embrasures of adobe had been built on the flat roofs all around for the harquebusiers, with two small cannon emplaced on their carriages at the main gate. The fathers of the parish church had consumed the Blessed Sacrament and removed the more important sacred articles to the fortress, including the beloved image of La Conquistadora.

Upon being ushered into his lordship's presence, Juan saw another Indian standing submissively before the lord governor. He was a Quéres Indian from San Felipe whose name was Bartolomé Naranjo, and whom Juan knew to be a very good Christian, like himself. Naranjo spent long periods working for the Spaniards of the villa, also residing in Analco, but had no family living with him as Juan did. They had long been good friends.

Don Antonio de Otermín did not look displeased with them, however, only very sad and worried. He promptly set the two at ease with his kindly manner and then his soft words. After quietly regarding Juan's open features, squarish and flat with the tone of old copper, yet not unhandsome in the frame made by the bobbed black hair underneath the bandanna—and then Naranjo's, also a sanguine face, but roundish and with a sooty tinge to it—his lordship began speaking. Three days ago, said he, he had sent a soldier to the lieutenant governor of the Rio Abajo, in order to ascertain if the lower valley colonists and friars were safe, and also to ask for men to come and help defend the villa. But the soldier had not returned. At the same time he had sent two Mexican Indians to investigate the Galisteo pueblos, and they had not come back either, although these Tano pueblos were less than twenty miles south below the plateau. The two Tesuque youths had told him that the rebels would attack on the thirteenth of the month; and this was Wednesday, the thirteenth of August, with only silence from that direction, although there was a rumor that the Tanos had killed Father Bernal and two other friars last Sunday.

Now, his lordship trusted Naranjo and Juan el Tano as he would his own brothers. For the people of Santa Fe knew that they were the best of Christians. Would Naranjo risk his life by going down alone to his pueblo of San Felipe, and there try to contact the Spanish *alcaldes* of the area? And would Juan do like-wise, by going to Galisteo to see if his own people had really killed Father Bernal and others? He might also find out when they were coming to attack the villa. His lordship then added that he would reward the two most generously on their return.

Both Indians accepted their errands readily. Juan el Tano, encouraged by the lord governor's humble friendliness, wanted to know something beforehand. He had often heard it said, even by the fathers of the villa, that the Virgin Mary herself had foretold the destruction of the kingdom some six years ago; as a matter of fact, he and his wife had worked many a time in the house of the late Captain Romero, who was the high sheriff, and his late wife Josefa—and he, Juan, had often seen the pretty little Virgin through which Holy Mary had cured little Maria Romero and made the prediction. Was this, perhaps, the beginning of that prophecy?

Don Antonio lowered his eyes. He himself had heard the story shortly after his arrival in the kingdom. The alleged miracle could well be true, since the fathers and the intelligent captains swore to it. But the prediction need not be realized during his present term of office, for he had always co-operated with the good fathers in abolishing heathen practices among the pueblos. Captain Xavier and the others had worked hard destroying *estufas* and the like.

But—aloud—he said to his two spies that, if that moment of prophecy had actually come, a Spaniard always died fighting. And they, too, like good Christian Indians that they were, should be prepared to die for the Faith.

Bartolomé Naranjo took leave of his companion on the out-skirts of Analco by taking a southwesterly direction toward the valley of the great river. He was in a bigger hurry, he said, because the distance to San Felipe was longer, and he was worried about his aged mother and two young half-brothers at their Tunque home near San Felipe, for they were fervent Christians also. Juan el Tano turned off directly south in a soft loping tread toward the much nearer Galisteo basin, and also thinking his own thoughts. His own parents were long dead. They had not been real Christians like Naranjo's mother, but they had been good people. His father had been a very great medicineman of Galisteo and his memory was still held in great esteem by his people. Folks generally feared the headmen of the secret magic societies, but they had always loved his father. And they had liked Juan very much also, because of his father—until he ran away from Galisteo to live in the villa of Santa Fe.

Many years ago, Juan had brought his young wife to the villa,

From Toledo

and they had stayed on as both had planned beforehand. For a while his people did not bother them, while the pair ingratiated themselves by their industry and sincere piety with the soldiers and the colonists, as well as with the Mexican Indians of Analco. Soon Juan was taken for granted as an *indio con calzones*—a trousered Indian living in the white man's way, for the men of the pueblos wore nothing but *taparrabos* or loin-clouts. When the medicinemen of Galisteo started coming to call him back "to do his duty for his people," as his own father had done for so long, the Mexican Indians hid Juan and his wife in their homes. And once when the *principales* of Galisteo went to the lord governor himself to demand Juan's return to his people, the fathers of the villa and many of the high officials like Francisco Gómez Robledo and Bartolomé Romero, begged his lordship to let the Galisteo couple remain in the capital. It was then that they gave Juan a little house in Analco with its little *milpa* where he could plant maize and beans for his family. He did chores daily for the garrison soldiers or in the gardens and fields of the officials, and sometimes inside the palace of the lord governor. His wife washed clothes in the little river, or cleaned house, or plastered walls with mud, for the kind Spanish ladies. Their little children were already learning their catechism from the father who attended the chapel of San Miguel.

It was a much more pleasant life than that of the pueblo. One learned about many interesting things which were real, not impossible tales about talking coyotes and spiders and turkeys which they had made him learn by rote in Galisteo. Many of the Mexican Indians had traveled as much as the Spaniards, and their evening conversations in Analco were a delight to hear; they also knew how to make all kinds of curious and useful things for the house, and almost out of nothing. In this new life a person owned his house and kept for himself the maize of his field, as also the little articles and varied items of food with which the Spaniards paid for one's services.

Of course, one had to go to catechism and *alabados* morning and evening at San Miguel, but the sessions were short, and he loved to hear the Mexican Indians sing, for they all had the most melodious voices, not gruff throats like his own and other pueblo Indians. At Galisteo, when the frequent dancing days of the pagan calendar came around, one had to obey the *cacique* and other old men under pain of being flogged, and so leave whatever work one was interested in, to spend days and nights of fasting and vomiting in the *estufa,* or practicing the monotonous chants and steps of the *cachina* and many other dances. After a *cachina,* some other man could violate his beloved wife, and he did not like that. In fact, he had turned against his people's customs the day when, during a rabbit hunt to gather meat for the *cacique's* idols, the headmen forced him to cover a girl while the other young people stood around laughing.

The Spaniards had many fiestas, too, but here one laid off work to rest and be merry. After the wonderful music and singing in the parish church, there were games to watch on the plaza, like the colorful skirmish of Moors and Christians which the soldiers put on. There were the spectacles of *los toros* and *el gallo,* in which men displayed their valor baiting bulls, or reaching to the ground to grasp a rooster while riding their horses at full speed. The Mexican Indians themselves put on their own native dances, like the *matachines.* They wore bright costumes with many-colored ribbands and tall rainbow plumes instead of ugly streaks on naked bodies. Their mincing dance-steps were pleasantly graceful, and their music

From Toledo

lively and merry, and everything was addressed to no other god than the festive spirit of the moment.

It was true that some couples of Analco, and even in the villa itself, were unfaithful to each other. At least that was the rumor. But it was their own sin for which God had His punishment; they were not forced to it by the authorities or by tribal custom.

Messengers had not ceased coming from the Tano headmen. But of late years they had not bothered Juan too much. The few times he visited his own pueblo was in the company of soldiers, lest he be detained by force. His uncles and other relatives did stop in Analco to fondle his children with real affection. But he wanted these children to grow up in the Faith and the customs of the outsiders who had brought so many benefits to the land.

Juan used to think and talk about these advantages often, although he agreed with his good wife that the religious ways of the Christian were by far the highest benefit. Being a woman, she spoke more about these holy things. It was closer to his nature, as man of the house, to dwell more on such things as animals and tools. There were some objects he wanted that he would never be able to afford, while some others the Spaniards did not allow the Indians to possess—like horses to ride on, and guns with which to hunt. He had learned to ride on horseback when some Spaniards sent him out to round up their steeds in open country, and ever so often the soldiers let him fire their harquebuses at a target. If only he owned a horse and a gun, he could kill deer by the hundreds, tan their skins very soft as only Indians can, and with them buy fine cloth and precious household articles when mer-chants and traders came with the supply caravan from the City of Mexico. His wife did like to talk about those big and unbreakable iron kettles, about the bright basins and pans and ladles of hammered copper in the kitchens of the Spanish ladies. She yearned most of all for those hard and smooth majólica dishes. Because these cost too much, she and Juan had to continue cooking and eating from the pottery of the pueblos which loosened grit and sand into the food one ate.

Ordinarily, Juan el Tano would have spied two scouts lying in ambush behind a clump of junipers ahead, had he not been thinking of a horse and harquebus and the majólica dishes. Each scout had him fast by an arm before he knew it, but they let him go peacefully with them when he said that he was on his way to Galisteo on his own. As they came near the village, Juan saw the *cacique* himself, and his father's brother who had since become an influential shaman, coming out to meet him with words and gestures of joy. For they obviously supposed that he had escaped from the villa to join them. They began telling him how much they needed his help because he knew the villa so well, and also the inside of the lord governor's palace and the quarters of the soldiers, and most especially the daily habits of the Spaniards. But they needed him most of all because so many people of the three Tano villages of Galisteo, San Lázaro, and San Cristóbal, and those of nearby San Marcos and La Ciénega, did not want to rebel against the Spaniards. But they would rise if he, Juan, the fine son of a great father, and once a close friend of the despised padres and colonists, led them into battle.

A meeting was called by heralds grunting long and loud through-out the pueblo of Galisteo. In the clutch of his emergency, Juan had not said a word. He listened quietly during a council meeting which lasted all afternoon and far into the evening. Before out-lining their plans, the headmen and war captains took turns in re-

From Toledo

counting all their myths concerning their origin, like their coming out ages ago from the bowels of Xipapu, and their dances which were a repetition of the ancient visits of the good and helpful *xihuanas*, and, finally, the orders received recently from the great Po-he-yemu through his wise and powerful *teniente* in the far north. All this took hours and hours, for the headmen repeated each other.

When the time came, at last, when Juan knew that he was expected to answer with a long speech of his own, he surprised the old men by reviewing the much more benevolent visitation of the Spaniards to the land of the pueblos. Where formerly the Indians had nothing but maize and beans and squashes to eat, the white man had added many other kinds of grains and fruits. From their mission dispensaries, the fathers lent their people iron hoes to till the fields better, and iron axes to cut down very big trees for beams. And so the crops were much more abundant; the rooms of their dwelling were much bigger and more liveable, because of the long beams. The axes also split hard junipers for better and longer burning firewood, a great improvement over pulpy cottonwood branches that gave more smoke than heat. The fathers also lent them the mission horses to haul the great beams and to pull the fine iron plows. And at certain times they killed a cow or a bull, for the feeding of their families when deer were scarce or the snows too high to hunt them. From the cows also came milk for their little children, and to make curds and cheese. What kind of spirit, then, was this Po-he-yemu who said that the Indians should go back to maize and beans and squash only? Would he also have them kill all the horses and cattle, and the sheep and goats which the fathers had given each family to keep and breed for themselves? Were the horses only for the enemy Apaches?

Moreover, said Juan, the people of the pueblos had always been known far and wide as people of peace. Was it a good spirit who commanded them to kill innocent children and helpless old men and women?

There was a long silence, with everyone staring at the floor, as was the custom between rounds of speeches in Indian councils. At last, his uncle spoke. He said that they would not get rid of the new seeds which the Spaniards brought. They would not kill the horses and sheep and cows, even if Po-he-yemu did say so. But they had to kill their owners to get them. His warriors had already killed the soldier-son of the absent *alcalde* of Galisteo, and other male Spaniards, but they still held the women alive. He craftily refrained from adding that they had also killed Father Bernal and the fathers of Pecos and San Marcos who had fled to Galisteo for protection—for his nephew's counter arguments had made him more than suspicious. And yet, the young man was needed to arouse the people to war.

It then occurred to the wise old man that his nephew Juan might like to possess many of these things, since he spoke so glowingly about them. And so he reminded Juan of another thing that Po-he-yemu had said: every warrior could keep for himself whatever he took with his hands from the homes and the haciendas of the Spaniards.

At this, Juan raised his head, and his eyes gathered light as he looked into his uncle's. The old man looked straight back, then turned to whisper something to a young attendant.

A short while later, a horse was led to the door of the council room. The light of the bonfire outside made the white Arab stallion look as though it were made of fire also. The fine arch of its neck was like a rainbow. Across the saddle lay the trappings of

From Toledo

its dead master—the bright helmet, the fine trousers and doublet, the decorated bullhide breastplate. From the side hung a long sword in its shining scabbard, and there was a musket also in its long holster with pouches of balls and powder.

This was all for Juan, said his uncle, if he called his people to arms. And he could get much more by way of pillage when the villa fell.

Juan was already thinking of the kettles and pans, the majólica hardware, the tall carved chests and leather hampers bursting with colorful silks and satins. Yet, something in his heart surged up and broke like a red spray over his vision. It was not right to kill for it, the old men heard him saying as if to himself. Then he stood up and told them he would lead the people against the Spaniards if there was no killing done, if the lord governor and the other Spaniards were allowed to leave the land of the pueblos unharmed.

The headmen smiled craftily, but by this time Juan could no longer tell if the smiles were good or bad.

The advance toward Santa Fe the next day was slow, to allow time for all the warriors of the five Galisteo villages, and the Pecos, to assemble at a forward point. The furthest pueblos had received Juan's decision and call much later, and needed more time for dancing before they waxed brave. Besides, contact still had to be made with the Tehua and Tigua pueblos north of the villa. A wandering band of Apaches, although their ancient foe, had already agreed to come and join them for their share of horses, but had not yet arrived.

Early that morning, Juan's conscience had given signs of rousing, but, after he had put on the trousers, boots, and doublet, and the breastplate and the peaked morion, of the *alcalde's* dead son, and as he rode up and down brandishing the sword while shouting instructions to the various groups from the exhilarating height of the white stallion—which he actually felt dancing to the tom-tom beat in its great quivering chest—Juan lost any qualms he might have had left. Besides the gleaming sword in his hand, and the musket in its long leather case, he was also very proud of the bright red sash of taffeta with golden fringes which he had wound around his waist. For the lord governor and the major officials in the villa wore wide bright sashes as their sign of office. He did not know, however, that it was the cover of the missal-stand in the mission of Galisteo.

There was much dancing all that day among the low junipers between San Marcos and the conical turquoise hills of Los Cerrillos, which lay between the Galisteo basin and the villa of Santa Fe. The warriors who had horses pranced and raced all around, as happy as Juan himself. Two captive Mexican Indians, the ones whom the lord governor had sent to spy on them last Sunday, made their escape to the villa, and must surely have notified the lord governor that the Tanos and the Pecos were on their way to attack it. But nobody cared now, as the warriors danced and screamed all the rest of the afternoon and far into the night.

On Friday morning, August the fifteenth, they could not be held back any longer. They were egged on by the Apaches, who had arrived during the night and were anxious to get at the Spaniards' horses. Juan was carried along by the yelling hordes, and soon they were trampling the maize *milpas* of Analco. Those on foot went scurrying through the chapel of San Miguel and the homes of the Mexican Indians, ferreting for whatever household effects their owners had been unable to take with them to the palace fortress.

Juan saw a small troop of mounted soldiers emerge from the palace gate. They crossed the plaza and came in between the houses to the little river's edge under the tall mountain poplars. He recognized all of them—Romeros, Luceros, Gómez Robledos, and others—his former friends who had taught him how to ride a horse and fire a musket. They shouted his name, calling over that the lord governor wished to speak to him personally. At first, Juan suspected that it was a ruse to trap him, and then he realized that they had his wife and children in the palace. He knew that the Spaniards would not harm them, but it came as a shock, this thought of his family, for he had forgotten them since he had started riding the stallion and testing the sword and musket. What he feared now was that his wife might have turned against him for being a traitor, and what the fathers called an apostate. Yet, she would surely be on his side once more, once the Spaniards had departed and she had the pots and kettles and furniture, and especially the majólica dishes.

If the cavalrymen made the least sign of trying to capture him, his own spirited stallion would help him evade the trap. This was the right time, moreover, to convince the lord governor that it was best for him to leave peacefully with his people. And so Juan rode across the river toward the villa, while his warriors watched silently from the housetops of Analco and the higher roof terrace of San Miguel.

Don Antonio de Otermín came out of the palace on foot, with some officials walking in order behind him, while the mounted men who had summoned Juan stood by at a distance. Instead of looking angry, his lordship appeared more haggard than two days ago when he had spoken to Juan and Naranjo in his office. What had happened to Juan, his lordship wanted to know. Had he gone crazy? How could such a fine fellow suddenly betray his dear friends, his own family, and especially his dear God? He must have lost his mind, surely. But it was not too late to make good. Let Juan show his good sense and good heart by calling off his warriors, and all would be forgiven.

To Juan, high on his nervous white horse, his lordship's upturned troubled features began to look most ridiculous. The man was plainly afraid because he knew that the colonists could not withstand the assault of the united pueblos. And yet, Juan did not wish to see him or his many former friends perish. In spite of his proud possession of this beautiful stallion and the sword and musket, and whatever else he would gain by plunder, he did not wish to kill unnecessarily, and much less these good people. Straightening up in the saddle, Juan replied that it was now too late for his lordship to offer any terms. All the other colonists in the Rio Abajo district were dead and could not come to the aid of the villa, he said; he knew this was not true, but it would help to make up his lordship's mind. He added that the friars and Spanish families of the Galisteo valley were also dead—although he had forgotten, in the joy of his excitement, to find out for sure if Father Bernal and the other missionaries had been killed. He further demanded that his own family be returned to him, and also any Apaches held in captivity. He knew that the villa had no Apaches at all, but his new allies insisted on his making this demand.

As Don Antonio kept looking up at him with that ridiculous expression, Juan remembered a dramatic gesture which he had thought up the night before, not realizing that his thinking was

From Toledo

following a Christian pattern. He proposed sending the lord governor two flags with crosses upon them, one red and the other white. If his lordship accepted the white one, he would be allowed to lead the colonists away from the kingdom in peace. If he chose the red banner, it meant war to the finish and the death of all the Christians. He had spoken fairly enough.

Again Don Antonio made his offer of amnesty and forgiveness. Then, though slightly betraying a surge of anger, his lordship said blandly that the Spaniards would never leave the villa without a fight.

Juan el Tano wheeled his steed, splashed back across the stream of the villa, and galloped up to his impatient unruly mob with the lord governor's answer. Immediately a tumult of whooping and hooting filled the air over Analco. Some warriors began blasting raucously on brass and wooden horns taken from the choirloft of San Miguel. Those on the chapel roof beat the bells with stones to a deafening clamor. At the sound, the troop of Spanish cavalry rushed up to attack them. As soon as they came churning across the river, Juan aimed his musket and fired. Down went a Spanish officer at their head—it was Andrés Gómez Robledo, a younger brother of the *maese de campo*. At the gun's blast, the white horse bolted and threw Juan to the ground, then galloped back toward the plaza. Only because his warriors locked fiercely and bravely with the mounted Spaniards was Juan able to get to his feet and draw out his sword. But one of the soldiers parried with his own and quickly swept the blade out of his hand. Juan retreated behind his men, suddenly aware that the marvelous superiority of the white man's guns and swords depended mostly on the skill with which they were used.

He found himself once more a primitive Indian, in spite of his uniform and sash, fighting for his very life with the *macana* of a fallen comrade.

Perceiving that the immensely greater number of Indians was proving too much for the small detachment of cavalry, Governor Otermín came out to their aid with more soldiers. He was mounted, but this contingent was on foot. The other half of his entire fighting force he left at the fortress to guard the government houses and the people, as a wise precaution against an attack by the northern pueblos from the opposite end of the villa. Slowly, but steadily, his men kept driving back the captors of Analco, routing them from house to house and from the interior of the chapel of San Miguel. It was slow work, for a group of warriors held on tenaciously to a house until the very last man was killed. Occasionally, some of these Indians rushed out for brief counterattacks while the soldiers were busy flushing out their comrades from another house. The Spaniards, however, stuck close together, rushing one building at a time; in this way they kept their ranks intact. On the same score, the Indians were able to prolong the encounter well toward sunset.

Since the loss of his horse and arms, Juan el Tano knew that he was no longer the leader of his people. He had served the old men's purpose in uniting them as the son of a greatly revered father. As a fighter he was nothing. While he did struggle bravely, he further realized that it was every man for himself; not only were his fellows scattered, and hence easier to kill by the soldiers who pushed on in close order and without panic, but the greater number of his warriors lay dead all over the place. The fire-arms of the murdered Spaniards of Galisteo had been recovered by the soldiers. All the captured horses had returned riderless to the villa or had been taken away by the faithless Apaches, who fled as soon as they saw that the battle was being lost. No other Spaniard had fallen since

From Toledo

Juan himself had killed the *maese's* brother—which meant prompt execution for Juan if ever captured. A few soldiers who had been wounded more seriously than others had walked back to the villa. Governor Otermín himself had gotten an arrow where his breastplate did not cover him near the armpit, but he kept on at the front of his men. On the other hand, most of the Indian survivors were getting weaker from loss of blood. Juan knew that by nightfall he and all of his companions would be dead.

The sun had grown squash-orange as it lowered to touch the summit of the great western mountain of the Jémez, when a cannon roared from the palace gate. Immediately the lord governor and his men heeded the signal and hurried back to the palace fortress. Juan climbed to the roof of San Miguel and saw, to his great relief, more than a thousand Tehuas and Tiguas coming over the northern hills beyond the villa. They looked like an army of ants rushing down an embankment, spilling down over the juniper slopes now glowing red from the setting sun. Their combined high-pitched howling at that distance sounded to him like the shrill of countless locusts on a hot summer day.

The straggling survivors of his own beaten army were too weak and disappointed to cheer when Juan let out a half-hearted cry. Instead, they sidled off among the junipers overlooking the villa from the south, and worked their way to safer elevations near the Atalaya, from where they might watch the success, or the failure, of the northern pueblos. Juan slunk silently after them, no longer sharing their comradeship. They were just tired and beaten, more like dumb animals licking their wounds, while his own wounds and weariness went deeper into his inner self.

* *   * *   * *   * *   * *   * *   * *

The Lady

Night fell in earnest all around, black as the inside of a great *estufa*, except for a blazing hole of light where the villa stood. With all the Spaniards barricaded inside the government buildings, the northern invaders had proceeded to set fire to the parish church and several of the abandoned dwellings by the plaza. Above their purpose to destroy was their need of light to keep the witches of night at a distance, as well as to keep watch on the Spaniards, who had no such fear, and so might make sneak counter-attacks in the dark.

Still clutching his bloody war club, its clammy handle as if glued inside his fist by the sticky gore of the day's battle, Juan el Tano trudged down the slope to see for himself. He also intended to report to the northern headmen on the bravery shown by his own people, as also to find out why these allies had come so late. He came upon warriors by the hundreds, still brave and fresh for not having fought at all. They were carousing and dancing where the fire blazed its brightest around the tall church. Some were roasting a horse which had been mortally wounded during the day's battle. No one paid attention to him, except for passing glances at the boots and the tattered uniform he was still wearing; but they did not look with too much curiosity, for several of them, though trouserless, had on brass or leather breastplates stripped from Spaniards whom they had killed days ago in the northern haciendas.

Confident that the Spaniards could be starved out within a few days, and valiant in the immense crackling firelight that made the night over the villa like day, jeering groups of them went hopping in unison up to the palace, but well beyond musket shot, singing mission hymns with the most obscene gestures. Others with blood-curdling yells taunted the lord governor and the watchmen on the palace roof with the death of their God and their Mother Mary,

From Toledo

and with the triumph of Po-he-yemu. But Juan recalled that he and his people had been just as confident, and yet their much superior numbers had been no match against a few Spaniards skilled in waging war without panic, and who did not have to dance beforehand in order to pluck up their courage. Yet, whether the northern pueblos won or lost, he would no longer share in the booty. He had so easily acquired what he had most coveted for himself—the only reason for his defection from his Spanish friends—and had lost horse, musket, and sword in one short moment. Even if his wife and children ever came back to him, there would be no fine cloths nor copper pans nor the pretty majólica dishes.

With these thoughts he went foraging half-heartedly through some of the houses which had not yet been set afire. But the new invaders had already looted whatever effects the owners had not been able to carry with them into the palace compound.

The house of the late Captain Romero, the former high sheriff, where Juan and his wife had often worked, admiring so many fine things, was just as empty. But in one room, lit up somewhat by the burning church through the opening from which the wooden door had been yanked out for feeding the bonfires, Juan noticed a familiar little object on the flickering wall. It looked like a scared cliff-swallow clinging close against the lime wash of it with widespread wings. It was the little Virgin of the crippled girl in her shallow recess. Young Maria Romero must have left her there on purpose, trusting that the little Lady would let her home and the villa be spared, just as she had been cured of her withering sickness six years or so ago. What foolishness, to expect such a thing from an object so little and frail . . .

Juan el Tano suddenly raised his stone mallet and swung at the

disturbing object with the tight-eyed fury of a crossed child. So
light was the image that it offered no resistance to the swift glancing
cuff that first nicked the edge of the niche. It flew off to one corner like a wounded turtledove, the mantle stiffly spread out like
trembling wings on a wounded grouse, the hollow cone underneath making a faint ruffling noise when it scraped the floor. The
little head, bouncing noiselessly from the upper part of the wall
opposite, rolled gently over to Juan's feet like a wild plum dropping
off a tree. Juan stared down at it and raised a heavy boot. But
then Juan himself dropped to his knees shaking with deep-drawn
sobs.

After a brief while he pulled from his matted hair the sweaty
bandanna which had held his lost helmet firmly in place. Spreading
it out on the floor, he placed on it the broken torso and the de-
tached head, which had a small notch on the forehead and was
smeared with the blood from his *macana* and his fingers. Then
he tied the four corners of the kerchief over them, and went out
across the brightly lit plaza toward the front of the palace. One
of the guards on the roof recognized him and asked what he
wanted. Juan, drawing closer with open arms, tossed up the
limp packet, telling the soldier to deliver it to Maria Romero,
the daughter of the former high sheriff. Going back across the
plaza Juan ran into the strong arms of some Tehuas from Tesuque,
who had seen him throw something to the Spaniards.

They hustled him off to a house which stood over toward the
river. The interior of its large *sala* or parlor was lit up by
candle stubs left there by the owners. The white walls flickered
with the shadows of several hunched blanketed forms, the supreme
caciques of different pueblos squatting on the floor all around.
When Juan's captors reported what they had seen, saying that

From Toledo

they knew him for Juan el Tano, a notorious friend of the Spaniards who had left the old ways long ago, some of the headmen began asking him questions in Tigua and Tehua. Juan got the gist of the Tehua, since his own Tano tongue was a dialect of it, and said that he knew only Tano and Spanish.

A very big blanketed man in the shadows then questioned him in very clear Castilian. Juan replied weakly that it was true that he had once abandoned the old ways in spite of the pleas of his people, but he had finally returned to lead them against the lord governor and the Christians. Let them ask the tired and wounded survivors of the Tanos, and the Pecos, and the Quéres of San Marcos and La Ciénega, now resting over by the Atalaya. They would tell how he and they had fought all day long, and had almost been wiped out because the chief of Po-he-yemu had failed to come to their aid in time. Therefore, that *teniente* was false, for letting the peaceful people be killed while he sat in a safe hole in the far north land.

As Juan was pouring out the pitiful contents of his poor chastened mind, the *caciques* and other headmen looked meaning-fully from one to another, and then began nodding in silent agreement, one by one around the room. The culprit was already "standing in a circle"—the ancient ceremonial punishment of the medicinemen for those who forsook the old ways or blasphemed against the spirits of the ancient ones. Juan also took notice, and he knew what they were about to do, but he was beyond caring or wincing. He stiffened and glared back at the ominous faces in front of him, not bothering to look at similar masks of death behind his back and on either side.

Standing up and gathering close around their victim, the shamans pushed arrows from all sides into every part of Juan's body, drawing out the shafts with shreds of his inner flesh and of his clothing clinging to the gills of the flintheads as the body slumped to the floor. Then the huge sorcerer who had spoken in Spanish threw off his blanket. His angry eyes shone yellow in the flickering light of the candle stubs. Putting on a bizarre *cachina* mask which made him seem even bigger, he gripped the limp corpse with his powerful hands, hoisted it easily over a wide shoulder, and went out to the river nearby.

The Spaniards standing guard atop the palace roof saw what appeared to them at that distance, along the fringes of the hellish glare from the burning villa, like a fearsome dark giant with the face of the Devil himself. Big sharp horns stuck out of his great black drum-shaped head, which had large chalk-white circular eyes and a long toothed beak like that of a fish duck. The monster was hanging from a river tree the limp body of an Indian whom they recognized from afar, because of the Spanish trousers and doublet and boots—and the red taffeta sash— as Juan el Tano.

2. ANTICLIMAX

Two events were the talk of the town in El Paso del Rio del Norte, and inside its mission of Nuestra Señora de Guadalupe, in midyear of 1683. One concerned the decision of the lord governor of New Mexico to move the settlement of San Lorenzo up the river from La Toma to the safer outskirts of Guadalupe del Paso. The other was the appointment of Fray Buenaventura de Contreras as procurator of mission supplies and master of the wagons which drayed them up periodically from the City of Mexico. The first brought Fray Buenaventura into contact with something which thrilled his big ox heart under the gaunt but heavy exterior of his person. The second made him more aware, although it scarcely dented his hide, that most of the ordained friars of the custody did not like him any too well.

Fray Buenaventura de Contreras was a laybrother in the Order. Except for his lacking the awesome powers of consecrating and of forgiving sins, he was no different from the ordained friars in the matter of external dress or in claiming equal spiritual sonship from the meek St. Francis. This prompted layfolk to address him sometimes as "Padre," which might have excited some jealousy among the fathers; but this also happened often with other lay-brothers, and the fathers did not seem to mind in their case. Or did they resent his sharp skill in figuring, and his popularity with the soldiers and other rough men?

St. Francis of Assisi had made no provision for the education of laybrothers, preferring them to remain "idiots" like himself, when this term signified an unlettered person rather than one bereft of reason. The laybrothers were supposed to serve the altar and the friary humbly with whatever qualifications they brought from the outside world. The custom of five centuries had already fixed their daily duties to sweeping the corridors and chapels, making and mending cowls and habits, scavenging for food as well as planting vegetables in the cloister garden, and preparing the fruits of these two latter chores for the refectory tables.

Some laybrothers, like Fray Gerónimo de Pedraza of fond personal memory among the settlers, still recalled as the victim of a famous accidental pistol shot seventy years ago, had served the frontier missions through their skill in medicine. In the City of Mexico itself, gifted laybrothers had taught the Indians music, painting and sculpture, lace-making, and other fine arts, ever since the days of the conquest. However humble or hidden the occupation of such brothers, they were not to be looked upon as mere servants of the convent; on the contrary, their guileless and self-effacing demeanor was to serve as a constant reminder to the more learned fathers that they, too, had to reflect the child-like virtues of their Father St. Francis.

Although Brother Buenaventura had often performed the usual humble chores faithfully, he much preferred other less servile activities, like keeping neat accounts for the friary, or helping out in drawing up official documents when the fathers were overloaded with work, or too tired, or just lazy. He also had a knack for handling people, particularly soldiers and ignorant laborers; some of these had been heard to remark that he had the smack of the barracks about him. It was for all these fine qualities that the zealous and revered Father Ayeta had brought him along as his assistant almost three years ago, when the mission supply train arrived at Guadalupe del Paso just in time to sustain the fleeing colonists of New Mexico in their desperate bout with sickness and starvation.

From the outset Brother Contreras had impressed Father Ayeta by making the King's regular allowance for the custody go a remarkably long way through his expert haggling with the merchants of the City of Mexico. Under his calculating eye the valuable supplies had made use of every inch of space on carts which he personally approved as sturdy enough to withstand the rough three-month jolting journey to the custody. This piercing eye discouraged any pilfering contemplated along the way by the soldiers escorting the caravan, or by the wild *chirrioneros* whacking and flaying the ox-teams with tongues as long and as stinging as their

From Toledo

bullwhips. Even the most uncouth teamsters, who would have thought little of slitting a friar's gullet if they could escape the long fingers of the Inquisition, had nothing but the sincerest respect for this gaunt leather-skinned Franciscan *lego*, who made them suspect that he might have once been a tongue-lashing *cabo*, or corporal of regular troops, before putting on the long blue robe which, even when tucked up under the knotted cord about his waist, still got in the way of his long martial stride.

Fray Francisco de Ayeta had been superbly satisfied with his assistant from the start, and Fray Buenaventura knew it. Once in Guadalupe del Paso, however, the efficient laybrother ran into trouble. While Father Ayeta, as a former and greatly respected custos of the custody, and no less for being the father procurator general, was to all purposes independent of local superiors, Fray Buenaventura was bound by regulations to come under the father custos of New Mexico as well as the father guardian of the mission of Guadalupe. While Father Ayeta had been around distributing the mission supplies among the needy refugees of the colony, and helping the lord governor settle his more than two thousand disorganized subjects in new towns along the river, Fray Buenaventura had trundled along close at his elbow ladling out his charities. But when Father Ayeta went back to El Convento Grande to report on the Indian Rebellion, and later, when he went on shorter trips to Casas Grandes and other places looking for more beef and grain to feed the colony, the father guardian had restricted Brother Contreras to the precincts of the El Paso friary.

Of course, Buenaventura had flouted such meddling restrictions by simply going forth without leave to see how the people of the kingdom of New Mexico were faring, and most especially the faithful Indians who had come with them. He was most solici-

tous for the welfare of these humble people. There were the Mexican Indians and other castes of Analco, dispersed in different towns
and getting the least care. There were the good Piros, who had ac-
companied the colony in its flight and were now settled in nearby
Socorro and Senecú, both places named after their home pueblos
which they had abandoned. Then, there were the Tigua Indians
whom Governor Otermín had brought back from Isleta during a
hapless expedition two years ago, and who were living in a new
village bearing the same name. The Spaniards, if not watched
closely, were prone to cheat these Indians of their share in Father
Ayeta's relief, and it was his plain duty to see that justice was
done. He could not do it cooped up in the convent.

On one occasion he had as much as told some carping priests to
soak their tonsures in the river. But he did not think that this
should be enough cause for so much ill-will. Besides, he had
often helped his bitterest critics in straightening out their pitifully
jumbled accounts and inventories, and also in taking up those
tedious depositions from ignorant folk applying to get married. It
was natural for so much generously shared talent to draw the flies of
envy. Buenaventura remembered that this had been the reason
for his asking to be transferred originally, from his own province
of Jalisco to that of the Holy Gospel. Since his own group had
failed to appreciate these talents, he figured that the other, which
had frontier missions in Tampico and in New Mexico, could more
readily find a place for his gifts. The father provincial of the Holy
Gospel accepted him provisionally, on three years' trial. And soon
after he came to El Convento Grande, where he began demon-
strating his capabilities, good Father Ayeta found him. Father Ayeta
was a man who recognized ability when he saw it.

And Father Ayeta must have rendered a superb report about

From Toledo

him to the father provincial when he went back to El Convento Grande in 1681. For now, on Father Ayeta's recall to take up the cause of the missions before the King himself, he, Fray Buena-ventura—and only a laybrother—had been selected by the pro-vincial chapter to succeed that great man as procurator and master of the wagon trains. While the fathers here in the custody might be displeased with this appointment, they should also rejoice that they would be rid of him for at least another three years, while he was fitting out another supply train in the City of Mexico.

Brother Buenaventura was already assembling his caravan for the return journey to New Spain, when he heard that the lord governor of New Mexico intended to move his seat of government closer to the town and mission of El Paso. Of late the wild Apaches and the Janos had been seriously plaguing his temporary capital of San Lorenzo, founded three years ago a good distance down the river at the place of La Toma. For the colonial government of the kingdom had continued functioning there as it had in the villa of Santa Fe. It meant that the exiled colony was being képt distinct and intact in order to return north some day for the re-conquest of the kingdom; this, in fact, was an end which Father Ayeta had foremost in mind, as part of the business he would plead before his Majesty in Spain.

As soon as the first teams of laborers, composed of Indians and some Spaniards of the colony of New Mexico, began working on the foundations for the chapel and the government houses of the new village of San Lorenzo, out toward the river from the outskirts of Guadalupe del Paso, Fray Buenaventura wandered over to investigate. He needed no by-your-leave from the father guardian now, since he was procurator general; and it behooved him to show his personal interest as a man of importance, even if his new dignity and authority had no say in the matter. While he was chatting with the *maese* Francisco Gómez Robledo, the grizzled officer in charge of the project, and whom Contreras had come to know during his relief work with Father Ayeta, a chance remark on his part opened new vistas to him that morning. The *maese* was explaining why the new chapel was to be dedicated in honor of La Conquistadora instead of St. Lawrence, as the curious friar had assumed. The officer's explanation was logical. Since Blessed Mary under this popular title had long been regarded as the Queen and Patroness of the Kingdom of New Mexico and its villa of Santa Fe, it followed that she should reign in the chapel of this capital-in-exile. The town's name of Real de San Lorenzo would be kept, to continue recalling that fateful day on which twenty-one missionaries and several families had died at the hands of the apostates three years ago.

All this brought back something to Buenaventura's mind, a faint memory of something which had impressed him at the time he heard it. While living in El Convento Grande, he had been told of a miraculous Virgin which had foretold the destruction of the custody and the kingdom of New Mexico. A certain Father Trujillo, whom all the friars of the great convent mentioned with reverence as if he were another St. Francis, had written about this prophecy of *Nuestra Señora del Sagrario* shortly after it occurred. This saintly father was stationed in an isolated pueblo in the province of Moqui at the time. He had also written that a little crippled girl had been cured instantly. When the supply caravan of 1680 arrived in Guadalupe del Paso three years ago, when Father Ayeta and his assistant first learned that the pueblos of New Mexico had recently rebelled and perhaps massacred all the friars and colonists, the letter of Father Trujillo had flashed briefly in Buenaventura's mind.

From Toledo

But then, what with all the work entailed when the southern and then the northern sections of the poor colony arrived, totally destitute and sickness-ridden—and then his own grave troubles with the father custos and the father guardian of Guadalupe del Paso up until recently—it all had lain forgotten until this moment.

Gómez Robledo explained to him that the statue of La Conquistadora was not the one involved in that miracle of the prophecy and cure. It was another image, one much smaller and less substantial, which had been brought from Toledo by his own great-grandparents. It was passed down through one branch of the family, that of his mother's elder brother, Captain Bartolomé Romero. The latter's grandson of the same name was high sheriff when his paralyzed daughter was cured some nine years ago, Yes, young Maria Romero was still living, said he, and in good health, down at San Lorenzo. Both her parents had passed away before the Indian Rebellion, and she had been living with a very old cousin, Catalina de Zamora. The *maese* believed that she still had the remnants of the miraculous image, which had been sadly battered during the siege of Santa Fe. This Maria had always been his favorite relative, the officer continued, but he saw little of her in the last three hectic years, what with all these futile campaigns into the kingdom, the troubles with the Janos and the Apaches, and now this removal of San Lorenzo from La Toma.

That same day the master of the wagons was down in San Lorenzo looking for the hut of Catalina de Zamora and Maria Romero. They were miserable hovels in which the exiled colonists dwelt, crooked cottonwood palings chinked and plastered with mud. Old Catalina began to wail as soon as Fray Buenaventura inquired after her niece and the broken statue. Without hesitation, Maria brought out something which she kept stowed away in a small bundle of her meager possessions. It was wrapped in a faded old bandanna, such as the Indians wore rolled on their heads like a crown, but it was neatly laundered. As the quiet young woman undid the knots over a low plank bench, the friar regarded her pale thin arms and her face with a real sense of awe. She was going on to twenty now, he figured mentally, from the year of Father Trujillo's letter. Yet, she looked healthy enough, in spite of the many hardships that she must have experienced at the time of the Rebellion and in the past three years. Her pallor must have something to do with the holy vision she had. Such a divinely favored girl, had the miracle happened in Spain or in the valley of Mexico, would have taken the veil in a convent long since. But here nuns were unheard of.

His reverie was cut short by the pitiful sight of the battered brittle remains of the hollow fabric husk of the figurine, and especially by the tiny separated head with its split forehead. Maria said that she had washed away the smears of blood upon it. Suddenly a swell of feeling flooded over Buenaventura's gruffness, his big mitten hands smearing a burst of tears all over his gnarled cheeks. This drew loud wails from the old woman whom the younger one addressed as her aunt.

Then the laybrother began telling the women about Father Trujillo of Xongopavi, how he had sought martyrdom from his youth all over the world, to find it in the custody of New Mexico at the end of his hoary years, just as a holy nun in Manila had predicted. Maria herself, who had never cried since her miraculous cure, also began to weep when she learned that this venerable martyr had written with such joyful anticipation concerning her own cure and the prophecy of her Lady from Toledo. But she promptly wiped away her tears and began telling her visitor how she believed

From Toledo

the desecration had come about. And that very night, she said with much feeling, the soldiers on the palace roof saw the culprit hanged by another chieftain who was very tall and powerful, and horned like Satan himself. But Aunt Catalina stifled her sobs to insist that it was indeed the Devil himself who had punished the Indian for his sacrilege.

The quavering wails of Catalina de Zamora had persisted all during the siege of the villa of Santa Fe, but they were the loudest ever, Maria Romero thought, the night when the soldiers brought Maria the broken pieces of the little Virgin in the dirty bandanna of Juan el Tano. Aunt Ana wept also, the very first time that her niece had ever seen her cry, but she barely made a sound. Maria, dry-eyed, blamed herself for foolishly leaving such a precious family heirloom—and what meant much more to her personally—at the mercy of the savages. But she had been so confident that nothing would happen to the little Lady, that her very presence would some-how avert the destruction of her home and the church and the whole villa. She did not stop to think that it was she who had foretold this destruction.

Afterward, Maria also thought that she herself might have faced the enemy with the little statue, like that brave St. Clare of long ago and the Saracens, but this was just a silly afterthought.

Her miraculous *Señora del Sagrario* had been Maria's only solace when her father and mother died some three years after the miracle. Josefa de Archuleta had really been a very sickly woman, and her daughter had begun to understand why she was so gloomy; but her outlook had improved very much with Maria's cure, and she died with a peaceful relief written on her features.

Her dear father's sudden death, only a few months later, was a much greater shock, for he was so strong, and he had not complained of being ill. Upon his return from an official trip to Galisteo, where he had gone to confession (Father Bernal afterward told Maria), Bartolomé Romero was sitting at table when he clutched his great chest with both hands and slumped over the dishes, dead. Maria recalled that she had not cried even then. She simply went to her Virgin in her niche and asked to be taken next, not with bitterness at all, for she was certain that the loving Mother in Heaven had provided for her good parents.

From that day on, until the Rebellion three years later, Maria had felt the presence of her parents at the little shrine in her room. She talked to them as well as to the Mother of God.

Aunt Catalina de Zamora decided to move in with her for her dear orphan niece's protection and consolation, she had said. And she brought along three little orphaned nieces of her own to the Romero house. It was Maria, however, who had provided whatever protection her old and young female cousins needed. As for consolation, Aunt Catalina had been hopelessly inconsolable from days beyond recall. Fortunately, for Maria's sanity, Aunt Ana Robledo had continued her long visits, and Maria went to her house when old Catalina sometimes became unbearable.

Well before the Indians surrounded the villa, when the lord governor herded the entire population of the villa into the great palace courtyard, Maria had more than she could handle, not only with the disconsolate old woman and the three frightened little girls, but with the once so brave and youngish Aunt Ana Robledo, who had suddenly gotten weak and very, very old. The fast decline began on the first day of the siege when her son Andrés was killed, leaving his widow with four little girls. Cousin Francisco placed his brother's widow and children with his own family, while he busied himself with the defense of the colony as commander of the militia. Aunt Ana had chosen Maria's company, and her son was confident that she would fare best in Maria's care. This pleased Maria very much, not only because she loved her "duchess" so, but because she was now able to repay Aunt Ana's infinite kindnesses to her when she was helplessly crippled.

Cousin Francisco's men on the flat roofs of the *casas reales* all around fought bravely for more than a week, some of them sallying out for a skirmish with the enemy, or to bring in water from the ditch flowing along the palace front. In this manner many a savage was killed while no Spaniard had fallen since Cousin Andrés died. The people crowded inside the compound attributed this to the intercession of the Holy Mother in her popular title of La Conquistadora. Father Andrés Durán and the other two friars of the villa had set up the parish image in the center of the overcrowded yard, reciting the rosary with the people three times daily, at the hours of the Angelus. Our Lady of the Rosary, the friars reminded the people, had once saved all of Christendom from the onslaughts of the Saracens at the battle of Lepanto.

But even though no other fighting man had been killed since the initial encounter with the Tanos and Pecos in Analco, the sufferings of the people increased day by day, especially among the old and sickly like Aunt Ana. Days later, when the Indians cut off the water supply by diverting the ditch in front of the palace, Governor Otermín spoke to all the people. The time had come, he said, to conquer the besiegers in one final desperate attempt, or else die of thirst or be massacred by the cruel foe. It all depended now on the mercy of the good Lord. Therefore, it was the duty of all to confess their sins, and then pray all night to the holy Mother of God as the Queen of the kingdom and the villa. At sunrise all his men would launch the one great assault.

Maria Romero then witnessed how the Blessed Mother, who had foretold the destruction of the custody and kingdom, but not necessarily that of the people themselves if they mended their ways, heard their desperate nightlong plea. There were two major assaults the next morning, one before sunrise, and the other shortly after-ward to prevent the surprised Indians from rallying together again. By eleven o'clock of Wednesday morning, the twentieth day of August, victory came. Fifteen hundred pueblo warriors could be seen scampering over the northern hills while more than three hundred of them lay scattered dead on the plaza and the crooked streets between the houses. Forty-seven others were taken alive.

In this action only four Spanish defenders had died. It was indeed a miracle of Holy Mary, Governor Otermín proclaimed publicly, and Aunt Catalina wailed long and loud in thanksgiving.

The forty-seven prisoners were lined up on the plaza and questioned by the lord governor himself, while the colonists and the animals refreshed themselves along the cool crystal river under the mountain poplars. Sometime later, there was much firing to be heard on the plaza, but not by way of alarm. Cousin Francisco later told Maria that the prisoners had made his lordship very angry by in-sisting, one and all, that their rebellion had been planned and caused by a giant who lived far to the north, and that this giant was the *teniente* of Po-he-yemu. Governor Otermín wanted facts, not fables, and so he had them all shot.

That same day a council of all the officials and captains was held with the lord governor and the three fathers of Santa Fe. According to Cousin Francisco, Father Durán was the most insistent in saying that the colony should be moved all the way to the mission of

From Toledo

Guadalupe del Paso, for all the crops had been ruined, and the stock of the settlers destroyed or stolen. The families would surely perish during the coming winter from starvation, if not from the revenge of the rebels. Most of the military leaders, influenced by him, also argued that the kingdom was already left defenseless by the wholesale destruction of the many colonists of the Rio Abajo. And so the lord governor ordered the few carts to be loaded with the meager provisions left, and announced an early retreat for the following morning.

His lordship had ordered that only foodstuffs, little children, and the very old and sick, be placed on the carts. In that busy morning's bustle of departure, the captain who was carrying this mandate to the letter refused to let Doña Ana Robledo take the statue of La Conquistadora on her cart. At this, Maria's older cousin, the spirited wife of a Lucero grandson of Aunt Ana's defiantly took up the beloved image in her arms, declaring that it was going along with the people; and she picked up the statue like many a mother clasping her infant to her breast. Maria herself had her own martyred little Lady, still wrapped in Juan el Tano's bandanna and tucked under her arm; since it was so light, she offered to help her cousin carry La Conquistadora. But this did not prove necessary, for, once out of the villa, while all the men were busy watching for Indian ambuscades and keeping the livestock from straying, her cousin laid the statue beside Aunt Ana Robledo.

All along the way the soldiers flushed out Indians lurking alone or in small parties, and who promptly ran away. Some few who were captured gave fuller accounts of what had transpired on the feast of St. Lawrence, the first day of the uprising. It was ascertained that Father Bernal had been killed at Galisteo, and with him the fathers of Pecos and San Marcos. And there were the friars of the Tigua and Tehua pueblos of the north, all martyrs now like St. Lawrence himself, who was the very first Spanish martyr of Holy Church. He had gone from Spain to Rome to serve as personal deacon to the lord Pope, and in Spain he was a national saint and hero. Both Aunt Ana, despite her weakness, and Father Durán, made much of this coincidence.

Yet Maria felt very sorry for these recent heroes of God, Father Bernal especially, remembering his tender solicitude for her own sufferings when she was a little girl, and how he had asked her with tears in his hazel eyes to offer up her pains for the sins of the kingdom and the welfare of the Franciscan custody. These thoughts helped her to understand why most of the villa's people had been saved while the friars were not. Layfolk she knew had really improved their ways since the Lady spoke to her and cured her, and so were spared; but, while death at the hands of the rebels was counted a misfortune among the ordinary people, to priests like Father Bernal it was a blessed consummation. She had no doubt that Father Bernal, especially, had wanted it that way.

Maria remembered crossing herself for entertaining a very unholy thought in this connection. Father Durán had escaped death because of the simple fact that he was stationed in the villa, and not at San Ildefonso with the Indians. Five years before, as the missionary of that pueblo, he had frantically reported that his Indians were trying to kill him by means of witchcraft. This happened some months after Maria's cure and the prophecy. She clearly recalled that as a consequence four medicinemen had been hanged and many others imprisoned.

Down below the great plateau, along the rushing muddy waters of the great Rio del Norte—the first time Maria had seen it, and which made her think of the river Tajo flowing around the

From Toledo

great city of Toledo—the fugitive colony came upon more grue-some evidences of carnage and sacrilege. From Santo Domingo south through San Felipe to the hacienda of Angostura, they came upon the corpses of slain missionaries and other people. A captured Indian told how the Indians of San Felipe had killed one of their own, whose name was Bartolomé Naranjo. When Naranjo arrived at the pueblo and found his people dancing as for war, he upbraided them for their apostasy, and the medicinemen chopped him down with their *macanas*. Maria and others recalled that it was this man whom Governor Otermín had sent out to spy on San Felipe, on the same day that he dispatched Juan el Tano to his pueblo of Galisteo. Good and faithful Naranjo had died for the Faith, while Juan el Tano had turned into an apostate.

And still, Maria was sure that Juan had redeemed himself through repentance, recalling his piety when he and his wife visited her Lady from Toledo in her room. If it was the devil who had hanged him, it must have been because Juan was truly sorry. Otherwise, the act had no meaning.

Already filled with bitterness at the sight of so much slaughter, the refugees from Santa Fe were greatly angered upon discovering that most of the colonists of Bernalillo and neighboring haciendas of the lower valley were not dead, but had fled south to Isleta instead of coming to the aid of the villa. At Isleta they discovered that these people had continued fleeing all the way down to Guadalupe del Paso. Nor was their anger assuaged by the testi-mony of other captured Indians, who said that they had made these Rio Abajo colonists believe that the villa and all the Spaniards of the north had been wiped out on the very first day of the Rebellion.

These witnesses also verified the massacre of the helpless fathers at Jémez, Acoma, Zuñi—and also of those in the faraway Moqui pueblos of Aguatubi, Oraibi, and Xongopavi. In all, there were twenty-one Franciscans accounted for who had died on the feast of St. Lawrence.

Maria had never known the last three fathers of Moqui. But all of them must have been like Father Bernal, to merit the palm of martyrdom. She had heard the name of Father Trujillo, because of his saintly reputation. (Only now, from Brother Buenaventura of the wagons did she come to know about Father Trujillo's long quest and the prophecy of the nun in Manila far across the South Sea. Where the sorrow of personal family loss had failed, and then that of war and all its hardships, the knowledge of this holy man's joy when writing of her Lady's prophecy brought the tears welling up in her eyes.)

It took the refugees more than a month to reach the mission of Guadalupe del Paso, what with the carts' slow progress and the prolonged stops along the way because of the sick. The worst part of the painful journey was the dreaded Jornada del Muerto, which started below Socorro, and away from the winding course of the Rio del Norte, until the trail met the river again near the mount of Robledo. Perhaps because her ancestor had died nearby, the great barren bluff made Maria think of the great mound on which the city of Toledo stood, and the curving Rio del Norte at its base became the river Tajo.

The weary colonists halted to rest about a league below this bluff, at a spot which had shone green from afar, and which Maria remembered was filled with Michaelmas daisies and other wild flowers. As soon as they stopped, Maria noticed that Aunt Ana Robledo was dying. If the siege of Santa Fe had worn her down to her real age, the hot jolting journey through La Jornada had sapped most of her strength. And yet the aged woman wanted to talk to her favorite niece after she had made her confession to one of the friars. Maria let her talk, for it made her feel better. Besides, no one ever thought of crossing Aunt Ana's will. Looking back at the great bluff, which she had missed seeing when she passed by lying on the cart, Aunt Ana kept on saying that it marked the forgotten grave of Pedro Robledo, her grandfather, who had died on the trail more than eighty years ago, when the founders of the colony first came into the kingdom. She was telling it to Maria as though it were a new revelation, something that Maria had never heard before.

Suddenly Aunt Ana stopped talking and went limp in Maria's arms. Maria recognized death right away. She remembered her dear father the day she raised his ashen face from the table.

That evening, a range of sharp granite peaks to the east were shining like organ pipes when they buried Doña Ana Robledo, while Catalina de Zamora wailed long and loud to the annoyance of Father Durán reading the prayers of *requiem*.

A year later, after the colony was more or less settled in huddles of miserable huts by the river below Guadalupe del Paso—the leading families, or what was left of some, having been assigned to the temporary capital of San Lorenzo at the extreme end of the settlements—Maria Romero at San Lorenzo overheard some soldiers talking about a scouting expedition into the abandoned kingdom which they had just made with the lord governor. They mentioned, among the familiar spots which they had passed, "the place of Doña Ana" near the mount of Robledo and about six leagues from the mountain called *"los organos."* It made Maria very happy to learn that her beloved duchess already had a place-name by way of a headstone, and so close to her grandfather's own natural monument, of which she had been so proud. Doña Ana herself would have approved most heartily.

Fray Buenaventura de Contreras had not been paying too close attention to the young woman's recollections, mumbled in what seemed to him a distraught monotony, as if her wits had been damaged by so many painful experiences. Besides, he himself had been busy meanwhile with a reverie of his own. It had occurred to him, on his way down to San Lorenzo, that such a heaven-touched relic as the little Virgin of Toledo deserved its own famed shrine, and the place for it was the populous valley of Mexico. The ideal site would be the great church of St. Francis of El Convento Grande, because of the luster which the heroic deaths of Father Trujillo and his twenty companions had bestowed on the province of the Holy Gospel.

It also had occurred to him that it was his very own bounden duty as successor to the illustrious Father Ayeta, to carry out this apotheosis. Not that he craved any glory for himself. But he could not help supposing that it would improve his own standing at headquarters. His three years of probation were almost over, and this could well mean his final incorporation in the province.

Nor could Maria Romero resist the entreaties and arguments of a haggler like Fray Buenaventura. With her parents dead for so many years now, and then dear Aunt Ana three years ago, and also because the crushed framework of the little Virgin's torso and her severed split head no longer bore any resemblance to *Her* whom she had seen come alive, and as though in a dream which time and misfortune had diluted, Maria betrayed only a slight hesitation at first. Then a vivid picture of old Father

From Toledo

Trujillo on the sky pueblo of Xongopavi rose before her—the saintly man on the lofty bare rock writing his touching letter, and six years later falling down mangled, like the prophetic little Lady herself, by the blows of a *macana*.

As Fray Buenaventura went on describing how the expert craftsmen in the *talleres* of the great City of Mexico would fashion a new sturdy body for the Lady, and restore the pretty little features to the loveliest perfection, fitting the head with a new crown of purest gold and vesting the new figure with the richest embroidered silks from Manila—and most of all, after he pictured the resurrected Lady enthroned upon the great golden high altar of San Francisco del Convento Grande for all the world to admire—Maria handed over her one and only treasure, although somewhat like a sickly and starving mother surrendering her child to the agent of an orphanage.

For once, old Catalina de Zamora had smiled and cooed toothlessly with a soggy tender pride, but her renewed outcries lasted for hours after Fray Buenaventura left.

POSTLUDE

POSTLUDE

¶ *The mission of Tlalnepantla, founded by the Franciscans sometime prior to 1580 for scattered Aztecs and Otomíes in the hill country near the ancient pyramid of Tenayuca, lay about fifteen miles northwest of the City of Mexico. Because it lacked a sacred attraction like the shrine of* Nuestra Señora de los Remedios *at Totoltepec nearby, or the more famous one of* Nuestra Señora de Guadalupe *at Tepeyac further down the great valley, the arrival of Fray Buenaventura in 1683 with the battered little Lady of Toledo proved to be a celestial windfall. Her story as the irrepressible "Brother of the Wagons" told it, combined the beauty of the Guadalupe tradition with the mysterious awe in which the folk of New Spain then regarded the far northern Kingdom of New Mexico. Nor did Fray Buenaventura hesitate to embellish the story with fantastic frills, somehow leaving the impression that he had been a witness of it all.*

¶ It did not take long for the statue to receive a new body, a somewhat larger cone than the original. The tiny hands, set into new arms, were then attached to the new frame. After the head was fastened to the new torso, the crack on the forehead was filled with gums and yeso, and the entire face repainted to look like new. Then came a little wig of fine hair and a precious silken dress and mantle (the first of countless others), and a miniature mantilla over the tresses surmounted by a crown of gold. A tiny gold scepter was fitted between the hands.

¶ The Lady from Toledo and New Mexico had never looked so beautiful and regal as now, especially on the day when she was enthroned over the high altar of Tlalnepantla. The town itself, suddenly become almost as famous as Totoltepec and Tepeyac, gloried thereafter in the many pilgrimages that came to render a very especial kind of veneration.

¶ For to all the native Indians of the surrounding countryside, her peculiar story elicited a sort of vicarious guilt calling for some form of expiation. This Lady plainly recalled them to a most heinous sacrilege perpetrated by a fellow Indian and his macana. The culprit was a member of a small unheard of tribe in the far mysterious north, true, but a place whence their legendary hero and father Huitzilopochtli was said to have come. Now, no Aztec had ever slain a missionary, much less desecrated a holy image. On the contrary, Heaven had favored their nation with the greatest image of all at Tepeyac. And so, their imaginations overwhelmed by visions of that northern Indian striking such holy loveliness with his war club, these Aztecs devotees had a little copper macana made, and then silverplated, in the shape that they themselves saw it—the great flint-toothed mace of their own ancient warriors.

From Toledo

¶ It caused the little Lady from Toledo to be known thereafter as Nuestra Señora de la Macana. *And then the patch in the nick of "her wounded" forehead fell out, and another dab of gypsum was pressed in and painted over—to fall out later and be renewed, time after time, and thus give rise to a further legend within a legend.*
¶ *Tlalnepantla's glory lasted undiminished for seventy years altogether. Toward the end of 1754, the Archbishop of Mexico withdrew the old mission from its Franciscan founders and made it a parish in the care of his secular clergy. The father provincial of the Holy Gospel begged to keep the famed little statue on the plea that it would serve as an inspiration to future missionaries studying at El Convento Grande. To this the prelate agreed, issuing a formal decree to this effect on November twenty-fifth. In mid-January of 1755, clutching her tiny scepter and her rather clumsy macana in her miniature embrace, the Lady from Toledo left Tlalnepantla in a memorable procession which wound its way down the wooded hills, and then across the lake-studded valley of Mexico, to San Francisco del Convento Grande in the heart of the City.*
¶ *In this same year a Novena with a brief "history" of the statue was published, for public devotional use in the new Macana shrine. Repeated editions of it, until as late as the year 1788 attest to the enduring popularity of both prayer book and shrine.*
¶ *History offers precious little after that, although we know that the shrine's fame perdured after the Mexican Revolution of 1821. As late as 1832, a Mexican lawyer investigating the distant department of New Mexico for his government, casually recalled the still-existent shrine in El Convento Grande of his native city; another Mexican gentleman, in publishing his memoirs in 1904, remembered how the high altar of San Francisco looked*

before 1861, on the lower part of whose tabernacle was a niche with the image of Our Lady of La Macana.

* *   * *   * *

¶ *As for New Mexico and Santa Fe, the scene of the adventures and mishaps which made the little Lady famous in a foreign land, the memory of her had faded fast since the day she left the exile capital of San Lorenzo del Paso in 1683. No traces of her remained in documents or in the lore of a pious people, as did happen with that other statue of Our Lady of the Rosary, popularly known as* La Conquistadora. *While the Lady from Toledo was a privately owned image,* La Conquistadora *was publicly cherished by all the colonists as the Queen of the Kingdom of New Mexico and its capital villa of Santa Fe; as such she returned in triumph with the glorious Vargas Reconquest of 1693, and has received uninterrupted homage ever since.*

¶ *It is only now at this very late date, and through these pages, that the Toledo Lady's own land of New Mexico and her city of Santa Fe, already a part of the United States of America for more than a century, become aware of her true identity across the centuries—and salute her across an international border. With the Toledo blood of the forebears and the many cousins of the High Sheriff's Daughter still coursing vigorously in thousands of her people, the salute is literally from the heart. Far less traceable, but there nonetheless, is the blood of the confused Tano Chieftain of the fateful* macana, *and even that of the Black God with yellow eyes, contributing to the salutation from the little-changed pueblos. All*

From Toledo

in all, it is as though all this happened only yesterday, even when the bodies of many generations lie mingled with the dust of those centuries. Ars longa, vita brevis.

[THE END]

HISTORICAL NOTE

For the inquirer who wishes to certify the authenticity of this true story, and to see how it was extracted from so many and varied sources heretofore unused, let him consult the article, "Nuestra Señora de la Macana," in *The New Mexico Historical Review*, Vol. XXXIV, No. 2, pp. 81-97, as appended to this edition.

And for the reader who is curious to see how the little Lady from Toledo actually looks today, let him turn the page.

Imprimi Potest: Very Rev. Fr. Vincent Kroger, O.F.M., Minister Provincial, Cincinnati, March 8, 1960. *Nihil Obstat:* Francis Tournier, Censor Librorum; *Imprimatur:* ✠ Most Rev. Edwin Vincent Byrne, D.D., Archbishop of Santa Fe, March 23, 1960.

NEW MEXICO HISTORICAL REVIEW

VOL. XXXIV   APRIL, 1959   NO. 2

NUESTRA SEÑORA DE LA MACANA*

Fray Angélico Chávez

A most colorful and intriguing tidbit of New Mexican history is
the image of *Nuestra Señora de la Macana* (originally called *Nuestra
Señora del Sagrario de Toledo*) with its own peculiar story. For this

---

* Literal translation: "our Lady of the Aztec War Club." This Aztec
weapon was a very large wooden sword, or mace, armed with big
flint teeth inserted on its point and along either edge. Spanish dic-
tionaries derive *macana* from the Nahua *macuahuitl*; yet, while con-
ceding some connection here, one cannot help wondering if it might
not descend from the Old French *mace*, derived from the Latin
maceola, whence also our English "mace." The mace was a common
European weapon before it wide use of firearms and the discovery
of America. The sixteenth-century Spanish of New Mexico still uses
macanazo for a swinging blow dealt with the clenched fist, or as
with mace. And Still, the roots of the Aztec word seem to appear
in the Delaware *tamoihecan*, the Algonquin *tomehagen*, and Mohican
tumnahegan, whence the English "tomahawk." The pioneer
Spaniards of New Mexico applied the term macana to the war club
of the Pueblo Indians, but this was a small and light stone mallet,
simply a roughly oval stone tied to a stick with strips of rawhide.

story is a most curious mixture of legend and history. Although both the statue and the story are intimately connected with seventeenth-century New Mexico, particularly with the great Indian Rebellion of 1680, neither was remembered by New Mexicans since those eventful times. But in Mexico City and its environs, the fame of the Macana Virgin grew from its arrival there in 1683 until the Mexican revolutionary upheavals of 1861; and even after that, until our own day, La Macana has not been entirely forgotten.

But, first, let us get acquainted with the statue itself, as it now exists in the ancient friary church of San Francisco del Convento Grande in Mexico City. It is a very old miniature copy of the famed *Nuestra Señora del Sagrario*, the age-long patronal Madonna of Toledo in Spain. This little copy came to New Mexico with the Oñate colony in 1598; after playing a fantastic rôle in the Pueblo Rebellion of 1680, it went down to the valley of Mexico to acquire a new name and its own peculiar fame. The Chanfreau photograph here reproduced was taken in 1957. It shows a small statue dressed in real clothing in old Spanish fashion. The relatively modern bronze pedestal, and the rayed metal aureole surrounding the head and figure, make it appear larger than it actually is. Between the statue and the pedestal is a horn-like wooden frame supporting the little torso which, as we shall soon learn, is a plain flat cone of wood covered with cloth, and not a carved statue in the round. On this wooden horn is nailed a silver crescent, the symbol of the Immaculate Conception, but which Spanish people used to attach to images of the Virgin without regard to their specific titles. Next to the scepter in the tiny hands is a stylized miniature replica, in wrought copper, of the Aztec *macana*. We also have, fortunately, a recent verbal description by an expert to complement the photograph: "The image measures 65 centimetres in height (about 25 inches), a little less than

From Toledo

a metre with aureole and pedestal (about 39 inches). It is fashioned in what used to be called *'media talla,'* that is, only the head and hands are carved completely in the round; the rest consists of a wooden frame covered over with cloth."[1]

As was mentioned at the start, New Mexico forgot this historic and religious treasure of hers almost three centuries ago. Unless some New Mexican of the last century had a copy of Barreiro's *Ojeada*,[2] the first one to apprise modern New Mexico of La Macana was Davis, her pioneer American historian. In his account of the Indian Rebellion of 1680, we find this comment in a footnote: "Among those who escaped was a Franciscan friar, who went to Mexico and carried with him an image of our Lady of Macana, which was preserved for a long time in the convent of that city."[3] Davis claims that he found this item in the archives of the secretary's office in Santa Fe; but this is so much like a footnote in Barreiro's work that we wonder whether it was a manuscript copy or a printed copy of the *Ojeada* which Davis came across in the Palace of the Governors.

Barreiro's own and very first footnote runs as follows: "Another missionary escaped to Mexico and carried with him an image of the Virgin, called N.S. de la Macana, which is venerated in the Convento Grande of San Francisco in Mexico."[4] This Barreiro was a Mexican barrister sent up by the infant Mexican Republic to make a report on its distant and little known Department of New Mexico. It is evident from the tenor of the whole report that the author did not get this information from the people and country he was describing; it was an item which he already knew as a citizen of Mexico City, addressed as an aside to officials there who also were familiar with it.

The able historian Bancroft, in criticizing Davis' garbled account of early New Mexican history quotes his comment on La Macana. Then Bancroft himself contributes new information: "On this image of Nra Sra de la Macana we have MS. in *Papeles de Jesuitas*, no. 10, written in 1754, which tells us that in the great N. Mex. Revolt of '83 ('80) a chief raised a macana and cut off the head of an image of Our Lady. Blood flowed from the wound; the devil (?) hanged the impious wretch to a tree; but the image was venerated in Mex. for many years."[5]

These enticing but meager bits of information were the only ones we had until the recent acquisition of a brief but detailed history of La Macana,[6] which was edited at the same time, and in the same place, as the Bancroft MS. Evidently a preacher of parts,[7] Fray Felipe Montalvo put his whole heart and soul into his Novena and History. After the first two pages of titles there is a short introduction (3-7) in which the author regrets the dearth of documents on the subject, and his having to depend on the oral traditions of his brethren and of people in general. Here he also discourses on the veneration paid to Marian images in Spanish lands under various titles; he makes his bow to the religious superiors who ordered him to undertake the literary task, and ends by quoting two *octavas* of rhymed quatrains to the Virgin Mary by a bygone Cistercian poet, Bernardo de Alvarez.[8] Then comes the brief history of La Macana (7-13), followed by the Novena devotional prayers and meditations (14-24), which are a set of cleverly wrought pieces to be said on each of the nine days of the novena, each orison a poetic play on several Marian titles in their connection with salient events in this particular image's history.

It is this brief history that interests us here, and which is herewith translated in full. Its detailed points are a mixture of erroneous his-tory and utterly fantastic legend, since Montalvo gathered his items from the faulty histories of his times, from popular tradition, and (as he himself tells us) from certain inscriptions upon a painting which depicted the Indian Rebellion of 1680 in New Mexico. However, with our modern trove of detailed documents on early New Mexican times, discovered in the past few decades and ably edited by various historians of note in our day, we can easily correct Montalvo and, in doing so, separate fact from legend. In this process, moreover, we begin to suspect that even the most outlandish legendary parts have a basis in factual history; in fact, we find the legend filling out historical gaps and throwing new light on the events of the Rebellion of 1680. Because of it, we might have to revise our picture of that Rebellion considerably.

To save time and space, but also to present the whole matter more concisely and in more graphic form, I have decided to place these corrections and gap-filling theories as editorial footnotes to Montalvo's own text, which is as follows:

BRIEF ACCOUNT
OF THE MOST HOLY IMAGE OF LA MACANA

In the very illustrious and Imperial City of Toledo, there its Cathedral Church, the Primate of the Spanish realms, has a Chapel in which Christendom venerates the Mother of God and most pure Virgin Mary with an especial devotion through a miraculous Image of hers, which they invoke under the title of *Nuestra Señora del Sagrario.*[9] The Reverend Father Fray Agustín de Carrión, in his sermon preached in that Holy Church as an Act of thanksgiving for a happy rainfall, relates concerning it that, when they carried it because of a drought from its Chapel to the main part of the august Temple, the Mother of God and Our Lady embraced it, for being a living portrait of hers.[10]

The Lady

The Franciscan Friars brought from Europe to this New Spain, as a copy of that most holy Image, and with its same title of *Nuestra Señora del Sagrario*, this sacred Image which we today call LA MACANA. And as their Protectress for their better safeguard on their journey, they took it to the still active Missions of the Evangelical Custody of New Mexico.[11] This divine Image belongs by tradition to the Friars of that Custody and the inhabitants of that Kingdom.[12] The Reverend Father Fray Agustín de Vetancurt wrote of the wonder concerning it, which he relates in his Chronicle of this Province of the Holy Gospel: *Theatro Mexicano, 4th part, treatise 3, number 64*, where he says:[13]

"Six years before (he speaks of the Indian Rebellion), a girl of ten, the daughter of the High Sheriff, and who was suffering great pains, commended herself in her paralysis to an Image of N.S. *del Sagrario* which she had before her.[14] Instantly she found herself cured. And in describing the miracle with wonder, she said that the Virgin had told her: 'Child, arise and announce that this Custody will soon see itself destroyed because of the poor regard that it has for my Priests, and that this miracle shall be witness to this truth: let them make amends for the fault if they do not wish to undergo the punishment.''

This conspiracy of the Indians came to pass in the year 1680, when the Christian ones, joined in confederation with the barbarians, rebelled against the Friars and Spaniards of that Kingdom, burning down the temples, violating the sacred vessels, and tearing up the vestments.[15] For they had been incited to it by the common enemy of souls who, as they said after being returned to the Faith, had appeared to them in the form of a giant, exhorting them to shake off the yoke of the Gospel and to serve him as their former master.[16] In one and the same day, and in distantly separated missions, they took the lives of twenty-one Friars and turned on the Spaniards who proceeded to defend themselves.[17]

Many of the incidents of this Rebellion can be seen on a large and beautiful painting which formerly adorned the Chapel of N.S. *de la Macana* in the Convent of Tlalnepantla, and today contributes to the decoration of the Chapel in this Convent where it now hangs.[18] Across that painting may be seen the bloody fury of the Indians killing various Friars. As the most vivid and ardent feature of the battle against the Spaniards, there can be seen toward its center a most beautiful reproduction of this most Holy Image, and an Indian delivering the blow with a *macana* on its head.[19] It also shows this Indian hanging from a tree, and at the bottom of the canvas there is an inscription relating the uprising of the Indians, their apostasy from the Catholic Faith, their attack on the Friars. And it goes on to relate, for a better grasp and understanding of the painting, what is transcribed word for word in the following paragraph.

The Devil, who visibly helped them in the war against the Spaniards, inspired an Indian Chieftain to enter a house where this Holy Image of Holy Mary was,[20] and which the Christians had hidden out of fear. Removing the Crown with an unspeakable lack of reverence, and vested with hellish fury, he struck the Holy Image on the head with a sharp *macana*, a weapon which they use. However, lest this execrable misdeed go unpunished, the Devil himself became his executioner by hanging him on a tree of that miserable battlefield.[21] After the Spaniards triumphed, and the Faith was planted once more by influence of this Divine Aurora,[22] this Holy Image was brought by Fray Buenaventura of the Wagons, a lay brother of this Province[23] to this Convent of Tlalnepantla, where it is venerated under the Title of Nuestra Señora de la MACANA.[24]

On each side of this inscription which gives the foregoing information, there may be seen among others, the two following

DECIMAS

Barbara accion inhumana
De quien fee no ha recibido;
Sin dispensar lo atrevido
De una violencia tan vana:
Al golpe de una macana
Hirió tan Sagrado bulto,
Sin reparar que su insulto
Mayores lustres abona,
Pues de un golpe otra Corona
Di a MARIA de mayor culto.
Pagó el Barbaro fatal
Audacia tan desmedida
Pues un Demonio la vida
Quitó con furia infernal:
Al punto el Cielo en señal
Una palma hizo hacer,
Que quiso Virgen vencer
MARIA, si assi se eslabona
La Palma con la Corona,
Por seña de su poder.

This second *decima* alludes, in the palm it mentions, to a luminous Palm that may be seen on the painting as though in the upper atmosphere; for a tradition holds that a bright and resplendent Palm appeared in the Heavens following the tremendous punishment of the sacrilegious Attacker of this most Holy Image.

The blow of the *macana*, for having been dealt less with blind anger and impetuousness than by a deliberate villainy impelled by mad fury, should have been enough to destroy the harmonious beauty of its Face.[25] Without in any way damaging its beauty, it only left a mark like that of a wound, though not deep, on the upper part of the forehead. And although at some time every effort was made to erase that mark for the completeness and beauty of the Image by filling in the cut and painting it over, its obliteration has never succeeded. For the red undersizing does not come together, and it is cast off by the more ancient, so that the mark remains patently visible; and this, in order to show in every way that this Holy Image is to be set apart for the especial veneration.[26]

Toward the end of the past century of 1600, various copies and portraits of this Holy Image having remained in the Kingdom of New Mexico, it was brought from the Custody to this Province with the pious motive, we may presume, of not being left exposed to similar impieties, and so that it may enjoy greater veneration.[27] Recently it was transferred from the Convent of Tlalnepantla, where the Friars had kept it,[28] to this Convent of Mexico, through the liberal and gratuitous donation to the Friars of this Treasure by the Most Illustrious Lord Doctor, Don Manuel Rubio y Salinas, Archbishop of this Holy Metropolitan Church—by his Decree given on November 27, 1754, upon the humble petition of the Province, after her Friars were deprived of the administration and doctrine of Tlalnepantla. The Holy Image was received in this Convent with the especial joy, consolation, and happiness of the Friars, and the singular appreciation of the Province, which so desired it. *Omnia desiderabilia ejus*, thus was the Ark of the Testament called among the People of God, the presence of which overwhelmed with happiness the family of Abinadab, and filled with blessings that of Obededon, the whole City itself partaking also of its benefits and graces: and what

I might call the total desire of this Province is this Sacred Ark, this Image of most pure Mary, in which we promise ourselves the grace of her mercies; and so to implore it, it was placed for nine days in the principal Church of this Convent, exposed to public veneration. Nine Masses were sung in its honor with all the solemnity possible to the weak resources of a poor family. A Novena was prayed to her Patronage, her Litany of Loreto was sung every day, and on the ninth, which was January 26, 1755,[29] it was installed, following a solemn Procession, in the Chapel of the Holy Novitiate.[30]

One must not pass in silence an incident which took place during the above-mentioned Procession. The tongue of a bell which was being rung by complete somersaults, and which faced the courtyard where the Procession was gathered, fell among a numerous concourse of people without hurting a single Person. The incident was considered so profound that the multitudes gave tongue[31] to the praises and glories of Our Lady, to whom all the ones due her be rendered throughout the world. Amen.

Thus far the brief history of La Macana by Fray Felipe Montalvo. To me, its quaint fantasy loses none of its charm after its elements of strange wonder have been pinned down onto historical facts. On the contrary, this dovetailing of lore and fact enhances the value of the legend as it adds to our store of historical knowledge. It also illustrates an old contention of mine, that folklore and history need not be inimical or contradictory, that genuine folklore is the poetry of history. And, as stated in the beginning, we might have to revise our picture of the great Rebellion of 1680 considerably, particularly with regard to the mind behind it all.

History itself hints that Popé, the San Juan leader, who is credited with the success of the uprising, was a rather weak character and none too popular with his people, to have united the various pueblos which were divided not only by language but by age-old enmities. Such a planner and instigator had to be a real genius, both as to his personality and his background of knowledge. Factual historical hints overlooked by Otermín and his captains in those crucial times, and now the subconscious recollections of the common people as preserved for us in a legend, point to that genius in the person of the black *teniente* of Po-he-yemu with his big yellow eyes; and he appears to be none other than the mulatto, Diego Naranjo, who himself had planned the Popé hoax to fool Otermín and his men and, consequently, all succeeding historians who depended on the *autos* of Otermín. (This solution is only a theory, of course, and offered here tentatively; students of history are free to weigh its supporting facts and their conclusions for what they are worth.)

As for the Macana statue itself, it likewise merits attention, for having survived and preserved its identity "so far away from home," and for such a long time, when similar objects have disappeared or else become anonymous in the turmoil of social and political change—and especially those violent upheavals which have marked the Republic of Mexico since its birth. The very fact that the Montalvo work was reprinted several times, and as late a 1788, attests to the statue's enduring popularity in colonial New Spain.[32] We read in the life of the Venerable Fray Antonio Margil, that indefatigable missionary whose sandals ranged from Panama all the way to Texas and Louisiana, and who died in the Convento Grande in 1726, that his body was disinterred in 1788 as part of the process looking toward his canonization; his remains lay in state prior to re-burial in the Chapel of Our Lady of La Macana, which at that time opened on the landing of the principal staircase of the Convento Grande.[33]

But even after the birth of the Mexican Republic in 1821, by no means anti-religious in its early decades, the Macana shrine was still well known. In his *Ojeada* of 1832 Barreiro mentions it as still appreciated in Mexico City. It was not until 1856-1861, when the Mexican republican government had been taken over completely by a European-type free-masonry, when churches and convents were "exclaustrated" (as Mexican officialdom calls confiscation), that the Macana shrine came to an inglorious end. The great sprawling buildings and courtyards of the Convento Grande were cut up into blocks and intersecting streets, when the chapel of the novitiate disappeared. This marked the disappearance also of that interesting mural described by Montalvo, which archaeologist Obregón tells me he has not been able to trace. The famed little statue, however, appears later in the church of San Francisco, the main church of the Convento Grande. García Cubas in 1904, from childhood recollections of the ancient monuments of his beloved city, describes the high altar of San Francisco as it looked sometime before or after 1861: "In the lower part of the Tabernacle was a niche with the image of Our Lady of La Macana, dressed in silk and her head adorned with a golden crown; she had in her arms the Divine Infant, and a little macana of silver, shaped like the swords of the ancient warriors."[34]

The ancient friary church of San Francisco, the mother church of all parish churches on both American continents, was converted to other uses by the Mexican government,[35] but it would take further study to ascertain when the Macana statue was removed to the church of Corpus Christi, where Garca Cubas said it reposed in 1904.[36] This church also ceased to be a house of worship in more recent times, presumably during the violently anti-Catholic regime of Calles (1926-1927), and it is now the Museo Nacional de Artes Industriales y Populares. Don Gonzalo Obregón informs me that the image passed on to the old friary church of San Diego, but he cannot ascertain when it happened or how long the statue remained there. Then it disappeared from San Diego, to be found later on in a house of (clandestine) Franciscan sisters in Coyoacán, near the southern limits of Mexico City. From here it was restored to San Francisco del Convento Grande by order of Fr. Fidel Chauvet, the father provincial of the Holy Gospel province; it was located for the time being (1956) in the sacristy of the Valvanera chapel of the venerable church.[37]

As these contemporary bits of information and the 1957 Chanfreau photograph attest, the little Lady of La Macana, formerly of Toledo, while heretofore but barely known by the name to a few in her native land of New Mexico, still refuses to be forgotten in the Metropolis of the Aztecs and the Viceroys and the revolutionary Presidents. On the other hand, her reconstructed story provides New Mexico with a fresh re-appraisal of one of the most crucial episodes in her long and colorful history. Incidentally, I have finished writing the Macana story at greater length in fictional form, as seen through the eyes of the High Sheriff's Daughter and the Black God of Po-he-yemu, in the hope that it will make interesting reading for a wider audience, if the book happens to find a willing publisher one of these days.

NOTES

1. Gonzalo Obregón, *Letter,* Museo Nacional de Historia, Mexico City, Nov. 10,1956. Señor Obregón, an expert on Mexican iconography, took these measurements for me. But he believes that the image represents the Immaculate Conception because of the hands folded before the breast, and that it cannot then be an exact copy of *Nuestra Señora del Sagrario de Toledo* as García Cubas claimed; *see* the latter's description of 1904 *infra*. The Virgin of Toledo, Don Gonzalo goes on to say, is an ancient romanic statue showing the Virgin in a seated posture and carrying

the Infant on one arm.—But here I beg to differ with Don Gonzalo on all points. I myself saw the original Toledo Madonna in the cathedral shrine of that city; this famed Virgin appeared to be standing because of the dress and mantle with which it always is clothed, and there was no Infant in her arms; and the empty hands were folded in front of the breast. José Augusto Sánchez Pérez, *El Culto Mariano en España* (Madrid, 1943), illustrates his history of the Toledo Virgin with pictures of the unclothed romanic figure, which is seated, and also as it appears clothed in the shrine; some pictures show it holding the detachable figure of the Infant, others show it without the Christ Child; *see* note 9 *infra*. Therefore, a replica or copy in *media talla*, and then dressed, could legitimately represent the Toledo figure as it is seen by the public; and it could hold an Infant, or simply the bare hands folded before the breast, *see* note 34 *infra*.

2. Antonio Barreiro, *Ojeada Sobre el Nuevo Mexico* (Puebla, 1832), translated and edited by L. B. Bloom in *New Mexico Historical Review, III*. 75-96, 145-178. The translation in the Carroll and Haggard edition of *Three New Mexico Chronicles*, made from Escudero's edition of Barreiro, does not carry the Macana item, as noted *ibid.*, 159.

3. W. W. H. Davis, *The Spanish Conquest of New Mexico* (Doylestown, Pa., 1869), 336n.

4. *New Mexico Historical Review, III*, 76n.

5. H. H. Bancroft, *History of New Mexico and Arizona* (San Francisco, 1889), 195n. This one-page manuscript, title by a different hand *"Sobre la Imagen de la Macana,"* was numbered as Number 10 in a group entitled *"Papeles de Jesuitas. . ."* It is by no means a Jesuit paper since it was written by a Franciscan residing in the Convento Grande of San Francisco in Mexico City, and at the very time Fray Felipe Montalvo was having his history of La Macana printed. At first it appears like a draft by Montalvo, but the spelling of *"Maquana"* and other radical variations point to a different author; these differences are pointed out as we go along.

6. Fray Felipe Montalvo, *NOVENA/ A LA PURISSIMA MADRE DE DIOS,/ Y VIRGEN IMMACULADA/MARIA/ EN SU SANTISSIMA IMA-GEN/ QUE CON TITULO DE NTRA. SEÑORA/ DE LA MACANA,/ SE VENERA/ En el Convento de N.S.P./ SAN FRANCISCO DE MEXICO:/ CON UNA BREVE RELACION/ de la misma Sacratissima Imagen./ DISPUESTA DE ORDEN SUPERIOR,/ Por el R.P. Fr. Phelipe Montalvo,/ Commissario Visitador de el Tercer/ Orden Seraphico de dicha Ciudad./ CON LICENCIA EN MEXICO:/ En*

From Toledo

la Imprenta del Nuevo Rezado de los/ Herederos de Doña Maria de Rivera;/ en el Empedradillo. Año de 1755.—A preceding title, probably the paper cover, has a wood engraving of the image with this legend beneath: *V.R. de N. Sa. de la Macana que se Va. en el Conv. to de Francisco de Tlalnepantla* (this last word is erased partially and *Mex.* printed over it by hand; then *Sylverio, S* unfinished or partly rubbed out). This correction, and some lack of correction throughout the text, show that the work was written at Tlalnepantla, and that parts of it had already been set in type, when the statue was transferred to Mexico City toward the end of 1754.— The first lead to Montalvo's work was found in Eleanor B. Adams, *A Bio-bibliography of Franciscan Authors in Central America* (Washington, 1953), 57, which notes that it was reprinted in 1755, 1761, 1762. Miss Adams luckily procured a photo copy from the Biblioteca Nacional, Santiago de Chile; it now reposes in the Archives of the Archdiocese of Santa Fe: 1755, no. 3.

7. Adams, *op. cit.*, notes three printed sermons of his: one on St. Clare for the Franciscan Nuns of the Court, 1748, another on St. Dominic for the Dominican friars, 1760; and the third for the dedication of the Hospital of Franciscan Tertiaries, 1761. Montalvo also taught theology and was a censor for the Holy Office.

8. A Fray Bernardo de Alvarez Morales, of Rebollar de Villaviciosa, published among other works, *Lustro primero del Púlpito consagrado a las gloriosas fatigas de Maria Sma.* (Salamanca, 1692). Cejador y Frauca, *Lenqua y Literatura Castellana* (Madrid, 1916), V, 300.

9. *El Sagrario* is a special chapel in cathedrals where the Eucharist is reserved. In Spanish cathedrals it also serves as the parish church of the faithful living in the vicinity, since the main cathedral is the mother church of the entire diocese. Toledo's Sagrario Virgin is said to date from the first century, having been brought there from Rome by St. Eugene, first bishop of Toledo. Since the image took part in the city's long history under Romans, Visigoths, Moors, and Spaniards, it has a national as well as a religious significance. It is a carved seated figure of wood, its contours having been covered with silver sheets following the discovery of America. The Infant is detachable. Since the figure is always dressed in a conical dress and mantle according to a very old Spanish fashion, it appears to be standing; old engravings and modern photographs show it with or without the Infant. Sánchez Pérez, *Culto Mariano, see* note 1 *supra.*—A charming but little known master-piece of Toledo's great master, El Greco, shows this statue with St. Ildefonso, Archbishop of Toledo (659-668); legend holds that the Virgin Mary herself appeared to this

saint to invest him with a chasuble, and in doing so she touched the famed statue with her person. The painting now hangs in the hospital Illescas near Toledo.

10. Fray Agustín Carrión Ponce y Molina was a Franciscan writer who published his *Sermones varios de festividades de N.Sa. y Santos,* Toledo, 1654, 1660. Cejador y Frauca, op. cit., V, 214.—Perhaps Montalvo, if not Carrión himself, telescoped the miracle of the rain with that of St. Ildefonso in the foregoing note.

11. The Custody of the Conversion of St. Paul in New Mexico was a filial body of the Franciscan Province of the Holy Gospel, which had its headquarters at El Convento Grande de San Francisco in Mexico City.

12. Montalvo and the anonymous author of the Bancroft MS have hazy and erroneous ideas about the founding of the New Mexico colony and missions. Had they consulted the Viceroy's archives nearby, they could have made use of the original Oñate reports, ably edited in our times by George P. Hammond in his two-volume *Don Juan de Oñate, Colonizer of New Mexico, 1595-1628* (Albuquerque, 1953). Or a careful systematic search in their own friary's archive might have thrown considerable light on the pioneer missionaries who went with Oñate. The Bancroft MS states, and Montalvo implies it, that a group of friars from Spain went directly to New Mexico with the image, but when they went or who they were he cannot say, because documents are lacking due to the hardships of those times and the scarcity of paper.—But we now know that no friars ever went to New Mexico directly from Spain; some of those pioneers were natives of different parts of Spain while others were creoles of New Spain, and all were processed through headquarters of the Holy Gospel in Mexico City. That the statue belonged to the Franciscan missions, or to the colony as a whole, is belied by what follows.

13. Vetancurt's work was printed in Mexico City, 1697, 1698; it was reprinted in four volumes, *Biblioteca Histórica de la Iberia* (Mexico, 1870-71). Vetancurt says that he got the item of the miraculous cure and prophecy from a letter written to a friar of the Convento Grande by Fray José de Trujillo, the missionary of the Moqui pueblo of Xongopavi in that year of 1674; in his sketch of Father Trujillo, Vetancurt says that this friar had sought martyrdom in Japan, but was told by the holy nun in Manila that he would find it in New Mexico. Some forty years later, the aged Father Trujillo attained his goal in the catastrophe which was foretold, for he was martyred at Xongopavi on August 10, 1680.—The Bancroft MS does not relate this item of the crippled girl and the prophecy. As Montalvo says, he got it from Vetancurt, although his supposedly direct quotation varies some-

From Toledo

what because of a comma: *Seis años antes (habla de la rebelion de los Indios) una Niña de diez años, hija del Alguacil Mayor, que estaba con graves dolores, tullida se encomendó*. . . This is Vetancurt's account: *Seis años antes, una niña de diez (hija del alguacil mayor que estaba con graves dolores tullida) se encomendó a una imágen de nuestra Señora del Sagrario de Toledo que tenía presente, y subitamente se halló sana; y admirando el milagro, dijo que la Virgen le habia dicho: "Niña levántate y dí que esta Custodia presto se verá destruida por la poca reverencia que a mis sacerdotes se tiene, y que este milagro será el testimonio de esta verdad; que se enmienden de la culpa si no quieren experimentar el castigo."* And he promptly adds: *Publicose el caso, y cantose una misa con sermon, presente la niña.—Quemaron causas y pleitos que permanecian contra los sacerdotes en el archivo. Op. cit.*, 276-81. This same item is referred to in different words in *Biblioteca Nacional, Mexico, leg. 69, expediente 8, foja 2v.*

14. The term *tullida* implies a crippling from disease, not from some external accident, and in a child it suggests the results of polio or rheumatic fever. Now, this invalid girl had the statue in her presence, in her sick-room. This shows that it was a household *santo*, and not mission property. Such a tiny and relatively inexpensive copy was evidently a family heirloom; as a copy of a specific Madonna, if we keep in mind the custom of the times, it must then have come to New Mexico with a Toledo family. Now, there was only one such family in Oñate's colony, and none such came thereafter. It was the family of Pedro Robledo and Catalina López with their four soldier-sons and two daughters; this included Bartolomé Romero, a native of a village near Toledo, who was married to their elder daughter *Luisa*. See Fray Angélico Chávez, *Origins of New Mexico Families in the Spanish Colonial Period* (Santa Fe, 1954), 93-94, 95-98. The nameless crippled girl had to be a great-grandchild of one of the children of Pedro Robledo, but who was she?

Pedro Robledo died when the colony was entering New Mexico in 1598, and some years later his widow returned to New Spain with her three Robledo sons, one of the four having died in a dramatic fall off the cliff of Acoma. The two daughters remained with their husbands, the younger one having married a Tápia who eventually moved down to the Rio Abajo. But Luisa Robledo and Bartolomé Romero stayed on in Santa Fe, the capital and only Spanish town in that first century. By 1674, the year of the miracle and prophecy, their many grandchildren were numbered among the Gómez Robledos, some of the Luceros de Godoy, and the several Romeros of Santa Fe. The various adult male members of these families generally took turns at being major officials of the Kingdom of New Mexico, including the office of high sheriff. But which one was high sheriff in 1674?

The closest we can get is Bartolomé Romero III, the eldest son of an eldest son. He was high sheriff in 1669, according to Fray Juan Bernal, as also a *sargento mayor* and a Spaniard of excellent qualities (*Archivo General de la Nacion, Mexico, Inquisición, t. 666, f. 532*). Actually, there are no documents for 1674 and the years just before and after, a phenomenon noted by Frances V. Scholes in his conclusion to *Troublous Times in New Mexico, 1659-1670* (Santa Fe, 1942), 245-58, where he cites Vetancurt's version of the miracle. As Vetancurt wrote: "The news was published abroad, and a Mass was sung with a sermon, the girl being present. They burned complaints and lawsuits against the priests which had been filed in the archive." There is no reason to doubt that this is the cause for such an abrupt dearth in documents at this very time. Whether or not the miracle is admitted as such, or only as an instance of illusion and faith-healing, the fact itself cannot be denied. Anyway, we can assume that Romero continued in office for the next five years, and that his crippled daughter was a "Maria Romero." But even if Bartolomé Romero III was not the high sheriff at the *exact time* of the miracle, we can still take our pick among the many contemporary female first cousins in the Gómez Robledo, Lucero, and other Romero families. It does not alter the singular Toledo derivation of the heroine's family.

15. Montalvo's summary of the 1680 Rebellion is correct, and the one in the Bancroft MS which is similar, as is graphically evident throughout the annals of the Rebellion as edited in Hackett and Shelby, *Revolt of the Pueblo Indians of New Mexico, etc.* (Albuquerque, 1942). But there is irony in the fact that the predicted destruction of the kingdom and custody (the terms were used interchangeably by friars and colonists) came about through the people's efforts to "make amends" and co-operate with the missionaries. The chief cause of their "poor regard" for their priests, ever since the founding of the missions and the colony, was the question of Indian idolatry; *see* the Scholes work just cited and his *Church and State in New Mexico, 1610-1650* (Santa Fe, 1937). The Franciscans wanted the *estufas* and *cachinas* completely abolished, if the Pueblos were to be truly converted to Christianity; some Spanish governors and major officials had opposed the friars on principle, or when bribed by the medicinemen. After the miracle, the officials proceeded to suppress the pagan customs of the Pueblos, and these then arose in concerted rebellion.

From Toledo

16. This infernal giant is the really fantastic feature of the Macana legend. But if we read carefully through the *autos* of Otermín in Hackett's *Revolt*, we find the Indians continually referring to the instigator of the Rebellion as the *teniente*, or executive, of the great spirit Po-he-yemu; he was a black giant with yellow eyes. The Spaniards dismissed it as pure myth; it so angered Otermín that he had 47 prisoners shot for insisting on this story, instead of revealing a real human instigator. But to me this *teniente* had marks of a real person, and I began looking for one answering the description—a burly negro, perhaps a mulatto with large yellowish eyes. Previous readings of old manuscripts had left snatches of such an individual in my mind, and I looked them up. And there emerged the person of Diego de Santiago, or Naranjo, a *mulatto* from New Spain. As early as 1626 we find him as a young servant at the Tunque hacienda of Don Pedro de Chávez near San Felipe; Diego, in fact, is married to a San Felipe woman. He appears to be the same mulatto caught by Bartolomé Romero I partaking in a *cachina* orgy inside the church of Alameda pueblo. Then he disappears from the documents, except for part-Quéres individuals near San Felipe whose surname is Naranjo, and who are sometimes *referred to as mulattoes; see New Mexico Families*, 80, 241-242. We can presume that in the meantime Diego Naranjo has been hiding out in Taos for decades, having impressed the medicinemen from the start with his African voodoo tricks and his knowledge of the lore and language of Po-he-yemu, while his youthful appearance persisted as a mythical description. (For the identification of Po-he-yemu with the Aztec hero-deity Moctezuma, *see New Mexico Historical Review, I*, 350-58.) Then the previous attempts at revolt by the Pueblos, as recalled by the colonists throughout Hackett's *Revolt*, begin to have a unifying principle, for the *modus operandi* suggests the same planner as that of the 1680 Rebellion.

A year after the Rebellion, when Otermín led a futile expedition into New Mexico, his men captured an old Quéres medicineman by the name of Naranjo (the first name transcribed "Pedro" by Hackett), who claimed to be *eighty* years old, but who was still very agile; on being interrogated closely, he furnished full details of the plot, this time inventing three spirits to throw the Spaniards off the scent—the first and only time they are ever mentioned, though Hackett and others make much of them. Naranjo also revealed his close acquaintance with the Moctezuma legend and its Lake of Copala (this lake never mentioned before in these Revolt annals). He went to confession and had himself absolved of his apostasy, once again fooling the Spaniards, and also later historians, by shifting the blame onto others.—The

Naranjo part-Quéres individuals near San Felipe suggest his paternity, as already said, but also others in Taos. To clinch all, in 1696 a José Naranjo of Taos, sometimes referred to as a Spaniard, helped Governor Vargas repress another major rebellion; later he led pueblo contingents against the Apaches, and finally became *alcalde mayor* of Zuñi. By 1767, José Naranjo's son, José Antonio Naranjo, who was also a military leader, had wangled the title of captain from the Viceroy himself, upon claiming full descent from the conquistadores of New Mexico; but the New Mexico Spaniards protested on the score that Naranjo was not Spanish at all, but the son of a *lobo de yndio mulato* whose father, a Domingo or Diego Naranjo, had apostatized in Taos in 1680 and also had instigated the rebellion of 1696. *See New Mexico Families, loc. cit.*

17. This defense refers to the siege of Santa Fe in mid-August, 1680, when all the people of the villa and from the haciendas of La Cañada and Los Cerrillos were crowded into the palace compound for protection. *See* Hackett's *Revolt.* —The Bancroft MS mentions the memorial service for the twenty-one martyrs which was observed in the cathedral of Mexico, March 20, 1681, and the sermon preached by Bishop Sariñana. This sermon was published in Mexico City that same year; it was published in English translation by the Historical Society of New Mexico (Santa Fe, 1906).

18. This painting no longer exists, and Obregón says he knows nothing about it. It was done most likely in 1740, when a special Lady chapel was built for La Macana in the friary of Tlalnepantla, according to the Bancroft MS; then it was transferred to the novitiate chapel at the Convento Grande, when the statue went there at the end of 1754. As Montalvo himself admits, much of his information was taken from the inscriptions on this painting.

19. Only the Bancroft MS says that the head alone was severed, and that blood flowed from the severed parts.

20. For us, the house of Bartolomé Romero in Santa Fe. Here is further evidence for the statue being a household saint, and not mission property.

21. A New Mexican Indian with his small stone mallet breaks the little image, which Maria Romero might have left there to protect her home when she went with the rest of the people to the palace fortress. But who was this Indian? And why should Diego Naranjo (or the devil) punish him for such a devilishly laudable deed? Unless this Indian, having once been a pious Christian, repented of his crime and upbraided the rebel chiefs afterward. These killed him, and Naranjo hung up

his corpse from a mountain poplar of the Santa Fe stream as an example to others. All this brings to mind the person of Juan el Tano, a pious Galisteo Indian living in Santa Fe whom Otermín sent out to spy on his pueblo. But to everybody's great surprise, Juan returned as the chief of the Tanos, first dickering with Otermín to have him leave with the Spaniards in peace, then engaging the Spaniards in combat. Juan's army suffered complete defeat because the northern tribes arrived too late that evening; and perhaps he openly blamed Naranjo for coming too late. (According to García Cubas, the Indian who broke the statue lost his mind and began running all over the battlefield until he was hanged by the evil one.) To appreciate this identification of Juan el Tano with the hanged chieftain, read Hackett's *Revolt*, I, 12-14.

Bartolomé Naranjo, a pious San Felipe Indian working in Santa Fe, was also sent to spy on his people at the same time that Juan el Tano got his orders. But he was slain by his people when he scolded them for rebelling, although his fate was not known until a year later in Otermín's 1681 expedition. It is interesting to speculate that one of Diego Naranjo's sons died for the Faith.

22. The effective Reconquest of New Mexico by Vargas, and the restoration of the missions, did not take place until the end of 1693.—Montalvo most likely confused the public image of *Nuestra Señora del Rosario, La Conquistadora,* which figured prominently in the Reconquest, with the Macana statue; *see* the Chavez article on La Conquistadora in *New Mexico Historical Review*, XXIII. 94-128, 177-216. A similar error was made by historian Fray Agustín Morfi three decades later, *ibid.*, 193.

23. This Fray Buenaventura de los Carros was none other than Fray Buenaventura de Contreras, who succeeded Fray Francisco de Ayeta as procurator of the missions and master of the supply wagons. A good idea of his forward and stubborn character may be drawn from a few lean sources: *Archivo General de Indias, Sevilla, leg. 140; Biblioteca Nacional, Mexico, leg.2, doc.6; leg.4, no.28; leg.5, nos. 2,3; leg.9, no. 8; leg.28, caja 70.* He was the type of man to give a fantastic twist to the story of La Macana, and perhaps leave the impression in Tlalnepantla that he himself had been in New Mexico during the Rebellion, although he never served there as a missionary. Anyway, the mural painting and Montalvo imply that he was the one and only missionary to escape the 1680 massacre. The Bancroft MS, and García Cubas also, say that two missionaries escaped; here the basic legend as told in some quarters evidently included Father Ayeta with Brother Contreras, since

both were associated with the returning supply train of 1683 which brought the statue to New Spain.

24. Prior to its apotheosis in Tlalnepantla, the badly damaged statue had to be repaired quite drastically, and this throws light on a conclusion reached by Don Gonzalo Obregón: "The study which I made of the image leads me to conclude that we have here a Mexican work of the second half of the seventieth century, and therefore it cannot be the original image taken by the first explorer." In other words, the original pyramidal torso of sticks and cloth, what with brittleness of age, was so badly smashed by the Indian's mallet, that a new one with its horn-like base was made for it around 1684 in the *talleres* of Mexico City. Hence, we must conclude that only the head and hands, or at least the head only, is all that is left of the household saint of the Robledo family.—Presumably at this same period the little replica of an Aztec *macana* of wrought copper was made for it, and his popularized a new name and title which, came to supplant that of the Sagrario of Toledo. García Cubas recalled that it was made of silver, perhaps a mistaken recollection after some fifty years, or it might have been thinly silver plated at that time.

25. A direct blow by even a light stone mallet would have smashed the tiny head beyond repair. Evidently, as the blow swept the battered fragile torso to the floor, the head came off and got nicked when it struck the floor or a wall. Still, since the whole frame was so light, the head so loosely attached to it, the total lack of resistance would allow the head to receive the blow, or part of it, with only a nick to show for it.

26. This quaint legend within the bigger legend undoubtedly arose from actual instances when the new bits of plaster and glue fell out from natural causes. The Chanfreau photograph brings out a big lump on the tiny brow, indicating that the last repairer of the face put in an extra supply of plaster for good measure. But when this happened, or when it will fall out again, nobody knows.

27. As historians conversant with conditions in seventeenth-century New Mexico will testify, the reproductions mentioned by Montalvo were an impossibility, and most especially in the dire straights in which the exiled colony found itself at Guadalupe del Paso in 1683. Moreover, if this had been the case, the memory of the statue and its story would have persisted among New Mexicans instead of being forgotten.

28. The mission of Tlalnepantla, near the pyramid of Tenayuca about 15 miles northwest of Mexico City, was about a century old when the statue arrived in

1683; for dates on it, *see* George Kubler, *Mexican Architecture of the Sixteenth Century* (New Haven, 1948). According to the Bancroft MS, La Macana stayed in the mission church for 57 years [1683-1740], until a special chapel was built for it within the precincts of the friary itself in 1740; here it stayed for 14 years, until 1754, when it was transferred to the Convento Grande in Mexico City.

29. The feast of the Conversion of St. Paul, which was the patronal title of the Franciscan Custody of New Mexico.

30. For a general plan of the Convento Grande, see Montgomery, Brew, and Smith, *Franciscan Awatovi* (Cambridge, 1949), 260; *see also* Garca Cubas, op.cit., and Fr. Fidel Chauvet, O.F.M., "The Church of San Francisco in Mexico City," in The Americas, VII, 13-30.

31. *El concurso se hacía lenguas,* a pun on the preceding bell's tongue, *la lengua de una esquila.*

32. Fray Pedro Navarrete, an outstanding churchman of his day, was signally devoted to Our Lady of La Macana when the shrine was at Tlalnepantla. Fray Francisco Antonio de la Rosa Figueroa, *Bezerro General, etc.,* Ayer MSS (Chicago), 40-41. This author also mentions La Macana when repeating Vetancurt's accounts of the Rebellion and of Father Trujillo.

33. Eduardo Enriques Ríos, *Fray Antonio Margil de Jesús* (Mexico, 1941), 193-95.

34. Antonio García Cubas, *El Libro de mis Recuerdos* (Mexico, 1904), 64. The presence of an Infant seems to be a mistaken recollection of García Cubas, although the old devotees might have made one for the famous Lady, to be carried by her on occasion as in the case of the original Virgin of Toledo; *see* note 24.—His account of early New Mexico is taken from faulty histories of the times. His version of the Macana legend seems to be a mixture of Montalvo and the Bancroft MS as relayed in other sources that he might have read. Accompanying his text are much too small and poorly reproduced pictures of the statue and of the high alter of San Francisco.—Rubén Vargas, *Historia del Culto de Maria en Iberoamrica* (Buenos Aires, 1947), 220, states that the image was a Corpus Christi, his information being taken from García Cubas.

35. Fr. Fidel Chauvet, *op. cit.* This is a good summary of the fortunes and misfortunes of the Convento Grande from its founding to our times.

36. Corpus Christi was the nunnery church of the royal Franciscan Poor Clares (*Descalzas Reales de Madrid, Capuchinas*); incidentally, these were the nuns who pub-

lished Montalvo's sermon on St. Clare in 1748, *see* note 6. The nunnery was founded in 1724 for Indian women of noble blood, and approved by Benedict XIII in 1727.

37. Obregón, *loc.cit.* The ancient church of San Francisco and the pitiable remnants of its great convent or friary were restored to the use of the Holy Gospel Franciscans in 1949; *see* Chauvet, *op. cit.*